the WAR ON SCIENCE goES BATSHIT

Allen J. Woppert

Acknowledgments

I would like to thank all early readers and reviewers, too many to name, thanks to whom this is a better book.

Barbara Derkow Disselbeck and Hannah Disselbeck provided invaluable pointers for tightening up the story. Science writer Richard P. Emanuel made a number of helpful suggestions, Richard Schluckebier gave me the encouragement I needed to go on, and Oscar Callupe kept my life in order so that I was free to write.

A special word of thanks goes out to my old friend and favorite paleontologist, Dr. Julie Dumoulin, for checking the scientific accuracy of the relevant contents. Any errors that may remain are, alas, my own.

A final shout-out goes to Eugenie Scott, Jerry Coyne, and others who, although they had nothing directly to do with this book, have been an inspiration through their tireless efforts to keep American science education mythology-free.

Chapter 1
A Batshit Family

My name is Timothy Thompson. I am 14 years old, and I come from Batshit, Illinois.

Batshit is a small place, and it doesn't appear on most maps. I suspect it is because cartographers assume it is a joke, but I can assure you, it is not. To the contrary, Batshit is a proud community with just shy of 21,000 inhabitants, 24,000 if you're talking "Metropolitan Batshit," which includes farms and tiny little clumps of houses within a 20-mile radius of "downtown." Batshit was founded in 1879 by a gentleman with the somewhat improbable name of Omar Batshit.

Omar was born in Persia, now known as Iran. He left the old country in 1866, working on a ship to earn his passage to the New World. When he arrived in New York, he dutifully gave his details as Omar al-Baht-Shi'it, single, age 19, occupation baker, but the immigration officer—either out of laziness or malevolence—transcribed his name as Omar L. Batshit.

There is much to tell about Omar, how he made his way to southern Illinois and founded a baking empire on baklava and Turkish delight. (Indeed, for those who want to know more, there is a whole museum dedicated to our founder, located in the huge, mosque-like structure that once housed Batshit Baked Goods.) When Omar died, he left his vast fortune to the town, which gratefully took his name along with millions in cash.

So you see, the town of Batshit has nothing to do with the excrement of a flying mammal. The name is pronounced baht-SHEET and, to the best of my knowledge and despite rumors to the contrary, there is no evidence whatsoever that the town's name has anything to do with the word *batshit* taking on its new meaning of "crazy." (If you want to learn more about the town of Batshit, I understand the town council is working on a website: www.batshit.com.) In the case of my family, however, take your pick on how to pronounce it when I say we are a Batshit family.

In describing my family, I'd like to start with myself, not because I'm so self-centered, but because I think you ought to know who you're dealing with. As I said above, my name is Timothy Thompson. One cannot help but wonder what my parents were smoking when they decided to name their son Timothy. I mean, really: Timothy Thompson? They might just as well have stamped "Tim-Tom" on my forehead at birth because that's been my nickname all my life, wherever I go. It's just too freaking obvious! Then again, there are advantages to having an obvious nickname. Nobody ever looks any further, and you don't end up with a moniker like Spike (although that one's kind of cool), or Zitface (definitely not cool), or Stumpy (just plain cruel), as some of my classmates are called.

But who am I?

For the sake of argument, let us assume for a moment that I am of above-average intelligence and take advanced courses in several of my subjects (where available). Let us also assume that I am a superb athlete, drop-dead good-looking and have a way with girls. Lastly, let us assume that only one of the above statements contains what could be classified as "the Truth."

As to the rest of my family, suffice it to say that the word *dysfunctional* was coined to describe it. Individually, we may just about be "OK."

My mother is what a magazine feature on her described as a "high-powered attorney, one of the Midwest's best." She is indeed, as the feature writer claimed, "strong-headed," "tough as nails" and "a formidable opponent." He was talking about her professional abilities, but I can vouch for those traits in her personal life as well. Fortunately, one further description from that article also holds true: "When she whiffs injustice toward any one of her clients, prominent or not, Veronica Langley-Thompson is as ferocious as a lioness protecting her cubs."

Now one might expect the lioness's husband to be, well, a lion. A paragon of fortitude. An alpha male. One would be wrong. Instead my dad is what one might call, for lack of a better word—and believe me, I've looked!—ineffectual. It's not that he isn't a good father—don't get me wrong. And I love him. He just doesn't know how to assert himself. In fact, he is—pardon my use of the vernacular—a wuss.

Now I would agree that there are times when a tactical retreat is called for. Self-preservation is always a good excuse for turning tail and running. As a frequent victim of bullying, I am an expert in this area. But I am fairly certain that standing up to my mother once in a while would not result in death or disfiguring injury. And I know for a fact that pointing out that a cashier at the grocery store has short-changed you also does not put one's life in peril, yet Dad is incapable of such bravery. Rather sad, really.

Our merry little band is completed by Goth Girl, my big sister. And I do mean big. If you were to see her from behind and were able to survey her massive shoulders, you would probably come to the conclusion that this wholesome lass has just come from pitching baled hay into a loft somewhere. Until she turned around, that is, revealing the full glory of her troubled existence.

It is hard for me to say what a stranger would find most disturbing about Goth Girl. Would it be the large safety pin in her right cheek, or perhaps the nail laced through her left eyebrow? Or would it be the pallor, which used to be the result of lovingly applied pancake makeup, but which somehow has become her natural skin tone? The black lipstick? The line of scars running up her left arm, where she likes to cut herself when she is nervous or bored? To me the emptiness in her eyes is what is most unsettling. The way she will turn her head to have her eyes pointing in your direction when you talk to her, never allowing them to focus or even move within their sockets.

I have tried to duplicate this effect, as I thought I could use it to frighten some of the brutes who prey on me at school. I have found it impossible to avoid focusing my eyes on something, and when I turned my head, my eyes always fixed on some point in my field of vision and failed to turn with my head. I have to assume that Goth Girl spent many hours perfecting the technique, and I truly admire her for both the perseverance and the effect, as disconcerting as I find it. So in a rather peculiar way, I look up to my sister.

[Aside: Perhaps I should point out that Goth Girl is not my sister's real name. We used to call her Mandy. My mother still does, but she no longer scolds me for referring to her as Goth Girl. My dad doesn't talk about her at all, and when addressing her he tends to use pet names such as Kitten or Princess, which I find even more ironic than Mandy.]

The four of us are rarely together. The exception is Wednesday evening, when attendance is mandatory. My mother decreed this after a visit to our family shrink, whom I will call Dr. Feelgood, with Goth Girl. Apparently the good doctor had diagnosed our problem as a family unit and prescribed more quality time. My ever-practical mother promptly called her secretary and ordered her to clear all late Wednesday appointments and demanded that all of us do the same. This involved considerable hardship for me. As president of the Chess Club at school, I had to reschedule our weekly meets, which had vast repercussions for the Math Club, the Debate Team and the Foreign Language Society. The girls' lacrosse team was forced to find a new water boy.

Goth Girl's hardship consisted of having to forego lying on her bed listening to satanic music one evening a week. This seemed trivial to me at the time, but admittedly it did send her into an even darker brand of depression, which was not lost on me or Dad, but which Mother was oblivious to. "Don't worry, Kitten," my dad encouraged GG, "it won't last. Your mom will soon start finding reasons not to keep this up, and everything will go back to normal." Her dispassionate "Whatever" was taken by Dad as a sign that there was still life behind the mask and that my sister might just "pull out of it."

Anyway, the Wednesday dinner event has been going on for nearly eight months now, and my mother is showing no signs of giving up. In fact, she comments repeatedly on how effective Dr. Feelgood's methods are and how much improvement she is seeing in the way we all communicate. To wit, here is a true and complete transcript of this Wednesday's fiasco:

Mother	Well, I'm glad you could all make it.
Dad	Of course, dear, I wouldn't miss it for the world.
GG	—
Me	Sure, Mom.
Mother	How long has it been since we all sat down for a meal together? A week?

Dad	Yes, I believe it's been a week, dear.
GG	—
Me	Yes, Mom.
Mother	And has anyone had any experiences they'd like to share with the rest of us? Mandy, how about you?
GG	— *[accompanied by a loud, blank look in Mother's general direction]*
Mother	And how about you, Timothy?
Me	Well, I got an A on my research paper on the effect of radiation bombardment on cellular thermodynamics.
Dad	Hey, Timmy, that's great. I didn't even understand the title, but I'm sure it was brilliant as usual. Isn't that great, Pumpkin?
GG	—
Mother	Well done, Timothy. Then again, we've grown to expect nothing but top marks from our son.
GG	—

[Time passes.]

Mother	The roast was very good, dear.
Dad	Thanks, Ronnie.
Me	Yeah, Dad. Good one.
Dad	Thanks, Buddy. You haven't touched yours, Princess. Didn't you like it?
GG	—
Dad	Anyone for dessert?
GG	—
Me	I'm pretty full, Dad. Maybe later, before bed.
Mother	I'm with Timothy on this one, Paul. I couldn't get down another morsel. Let me help you with the dishes.

The two of you can run along. I'm sure you have homework to do. Your dad and I can handle the cleanup.

GG   —

Me   OK, Mom. Thanks.

[GG and I exit. As my parents disappear into the kitchen with the first of the plates, I overhear the following before the door swings shut.]

Mother   I thought that went very well. Didn't you, Paul?

Dad   Oh, yes. We're definitely making progress as a family.

I would like to offer a few observations on certain aspects of the 55-minute conversation you have just been privy to. First of all, my mother is delusional.

Secondly, it should also be noted that I have never written an essay on cellular thermodynamics. I am not even certain that such a thing exists, and I do not know why I said it. Perhaps I will take that up with Dr. Feelgood the next time I see him.

[Aside: I have since Googled "cellular thermodynamics" and determined that such a thing does indeed exist. I scare myself sometimes.]

Lastly, the Wednesday night cleanup routine is always the same. My mother offers to do it alone with my dad for a number of reasons. Mostly it spares her having to prolong the sweet torture that is our dinner conversation. But it also allows them to be alone together. I often hear them cooing at each other in the kitchen like two turtle doves before disappearing to their bedroom to do things no son should have to overhear. (My room is right next to theirs.) I am not one for telling tales out of school, but suffice it to say that these sessions involve high-volume role-playing in which my mother is the submissive party. This I will definitely take up with Dr. Feelgood once we have dealt with the remainder of my early childhood traumas, probably in about six months' time.

Rounding out the cast of characters in this, my story, is an assortment of teachers, staff, school administrators and fellow students, although the word "fellow" implies some sort of, well, fellowship which does not in fact exist. Geneticists tell us that we share between 95% and 98% of our genes with chimpanzees, which is a full 95% to 98% more than I feel akin to most of the other students at Batshit High School.

Chapter 2
Welcome To Batshit High

The excitement and the hormones were palpable as I entered the gymnasium for the eight o'clock "Welcome Rally" on my first day of high school. We freshmen had to report early—the sophomores, juniors and seniors were given till nine o'clock to go to their homerooms. This was the Real Thing™, the big H, "High School" with no demeaning "Junior" ahead of it, and my friends and I were a part of it.

The bleachers were packed, with 372 eager teenagers shouting out to old friends, bevies of girls screaming as they related tales of summer romance, and nervous jocks grunting about why they ought to make varsity in their first year. The volume was nearly unbearable, and I sincerely doubt whether any basketball game played on the polished hardwood planks before us had ever produced this much excitement.

I quickly found my best friends front-row center, where all good geeks belong at an event of this sort, pens and paper or tablet computers at the ready. Josh Curtin, my best school friend, bumped fists with me as I sat down next to him and admired his new tablet. It was not really anything special, about two generations old, but I knew that he had probably had to cut a lot of lawns over the summer to buy it. His family was not so well-off, I knew, and he appreciated the comment. He was just about to show me his extensive games collection when someone started blowing into a microphone, ostensibly to test it, but actually more to signal to all but the denser jocks that this party was about to get started. A hush descended over the room like a pall. (I offer this simile as a gesture to Ms. Pewney, my English teacher.)

Another puff into the microphone, after which the puffer identified himself as Jonathan R. Powers, principal of Batshit High School. Several of my friends started the recording software on their computers. Since I have total recall, I had no need to do anything but listen.

Mr. Powers began: "Ladies and gentlemen, welcome to Batshit High School, the premier educational facility in Jefferson County. This is an exciting time for all of us here," he said, pointing to the assembled faculty members on the carpet which had been laid down to protect the center court. "For we are about to embark on another new adventure with all of you, our incoming class of freshmen. It is with the utmost confidence that we set out on this journey, and we look forward to another stellar year here at Batshit High."

I took an immediate liking to this man. With his words he made me feel special. For the first time in my life, I had been addressed as part of a crowd of "ladies and gentlemen," not as one of a bunch of "boys and girls." Mr. Powers had flattered us. He did not try to tell us what a privilege was being bestowed upon us in that the grand institution that was Batshit High School had deigned to receive us. No. He informed us that he and his staff felt privileged to have us! Yes, I knew, this was indeed going to be a stellar year.

Mr. Powers went on to introduce the department heads. I was most interested in Mr. Raymond Grass, the head of the science department and faculty advisor to the Science Club at Batshit, science being my best and favorite subject. My immediate impression? Totally batshit—with a small "b."

First of all, the man was, although the school year hadn't yet begun, already covered in chalk dust. Secondly, Mr. Grass's sartorial selection for the day consisted of, starting from the top, a rust-colored shirt that he had obviously slept in, misbuttoned and adorned with a pocket protector from Batshit Office Supplies ("Keeping Batshit organized since 1999"); corduroy pants in a greenish/tannish color, which, owing to the fact that Mr. Grass was obviously preparing for the flooding that will inevitably result from global warming and wore his pants several inches above his well-worn Hush Puppies™, revealed his Homer Simpson socks.

Thirdly, and perhaps most damningly batshitty, Mr. Grass wore an inflatable pool toy around his waist. I kid you not. The man had a clear plastic inner tube around his belly, from which protruded the long yellow neck of a smiling rubber duckie. This struck me as bizarre even for Batshit, but no one dared laugh. (I later learned that Mr. Grass regularly wears props to his science classes. The theme for that day was, of course, buoyancy.)

The last staff member to be introduced was Mr. Braun (pronounce it "brawn," as opposed to "brain"), who took the mic.

"My name is Mr. Braun, and as you can see," he said, pointing, palms up, all the way down his unnaturally muscular physique like a model in an auto ad, "I'm the head of boys' sports here at Batshit. Everybody knows me plain and simple as 'Coach.' Now my job here is to turn you boys into men, and to win games—but that's a whole 'nother story. So I'm hopin' that a whole bunch o' yous is gonna try out for football, basketball or baseball. And if you can't make the cut, there's always the more sissy sports like soccer and track. So come on out to the gym—that's this place right here—after school today for more info on the sports program."

Pardon me if I feel the need to make a few observations about Mr. Braun's speech. Firstly, while we could in fact see that Mr. Braun had an athletic build (to put it mildly), and could have guessed that he was somehow associated with the athletic department (the shorts, sneakers and whistle were definite clues, but the real clincher was the T-shirt that said "Batshit Athletic Department"), there was no way we could see that he was the head of the department. Secondly, and call me a prig if you will, I have fairly strong feelings about a) the use of English grammar, including things like adverbs and subject-predicate agreement, and b) the duty of a teacher, even one of physical education, to serve as a model for his or her students in matters of language. Mr. Braun's speech suggested that he had no regard for—or perhaps even knowledge of—the rudiments of correct speech. "Yous"?! That's Hicksville, not high school!

And thirdly, what to think of an athletic director who would describe such noble activities as soccer or track and field as "sissy sports"? But the main thought that was going through my head and those of my friends was, "If this person considers soccer players and marathon runners sissies, what will he think of us, people with no athletic prowess whatsoever?" I would find out soon enough.

The Welcome Rally, which no longer felt terribly welcoming, was winding down. We received instructions to line up at tables according to the first letters of our last names, where we would be given our class schedules and homeroom assignments. Except for a few of the more dim-witted, who were unable to cope with the concept of a *first* letter in a *last* name, we all did this and quickly and efficiently received the promised materials and, helpfully, a map of the school and instructions to report to our homerooms.

I am a good reader of maps; in fact, I have a Boy Scout merit badge in orienteering, earned over the better part of an afternoon spent traipsing around a field only to end up in precisely the same spot I had left three hours before. Maps appeal to my left brain, which is far and away the better developed half of my cerebrum. That said, let me tell you that the map of the "plant" (one of Mr. Powers' favorite words) of Batshit High School was—how shall I put this?—catastrophically confusing. Had I not been in a complete state of panic myself, I would no doubt have found it comical to observe hundreds of freshmen wandering the halls of the massive "Tudor-style" building, turning the pieces of paper every which way as they walked up and down halls, in and out of unmarked doorways and through archaic arches that looked like someone's rendition of the gates to hell.

When I found my appointed homeroom, the aptly named Miss Gaunt, who was to be my homeroom teacher for the next three weeks until what I can only assume was a long-delayed retirement, was the only other person in the room with me. This tiny creature had somehow managed to seat herself on a window sill approximately four feet above the ground, where she perched most elegantly, one leg crossed over the other. The smile on her face reminded me of the Cheshire Cat, for the rest of her, tiny as it was, seemed almost invisible. (If you don't know about the Cheshire Cat, I highly recommend reading Lewis Carroll's *Alice in Wonderland*. "I've often seen a cat without a grin; but a grin without a cat! It's the most curious thing I ever saw in my life.") I was ready to excuse myself for having entered what I assumed was the wrong room when Miss Gaunt beamed at me and uttered a heart-felt "Congratulations!"

"Erm, for what, ma'am?"

"For being the first, of course," she said cheerily. "And I do believe that's record time. What's your name, young man?"

"Timothy. Timothy Thompson, ma'am," I answered somewhat warily. Why was this enigmatic woman being so nice to me? I was, after all, several minutes late for homeroom.

"Pleased to meet you, Timothy," Miss Gaunt said and lowered herself deftly to her feet. "I'm Miss Gaunt, and I'm your homeroom teacher—at least until Mr. Powers can find someone to replace me. There aren't many teachers these days who can teach Latin and mechanical drafting."

I was unsure how to respond to this, but Miss Gaunt filled the ensuing gap before it could get awkward. "Now I wonder where the others have got off to… Ah, here they are," she said with genuine pleasure and wonderment, looking over my shoulder.

I turned to see two other freshies sheepishly entering the classroom, noting their relief as they registered that they weren't the last ones to find Room 421. I surveyed the small crowd as it assembled. Only one girl I knew semi-well, three boys and a girl I recognized from the halls at my junior high, and otherwise nothing but unfamiliar faces. Then, to my relief, in wandered my friend Josh, whom I'd been separated from when we had to split up by last names, him being a "C" and me being a "T." I had just started to smile at Josh when I noticed the pained expression on his face—not the kind of pain you show when you are embarrassed about being the last one to show up at a meeting place, but genuine, physical pain.

Before I could change my expression from "Hey, Josh, great to see you" to "What's wrong, Josh?" I saw the reason for the twisted look on my best friend's face. Attached to Josh's ear was a hand, to which was attached the arm of Robert "Bad Bob" Berg, the bane of Josh's and my junior high existence.

"It took you long enough, you little …," Bob was saying when he saw Miss Gaunt. "… genius," he finished, releasing Josh's ear.

Miss Gaunt pretended not to notice, but you didn't have to be an expert in micro-expressions to see the way her lips pursed in displeasure as she made a mental note about the tall, wiry brute who had just entered her realm. "Well, if I counted correctly, we're all here. Please take a seat, everyone."

As fate would have it, it was impossible for Josh and me to get seats together, and somehow I ended up sitting next to Bad Bob. No biggie, I thought. That can be corrected next time.

Miss Gaunt unwittingly put the kibosh on any such optimism. "Now, ladies and gentlemen"—there it was again!—"I trust you have chosen your seats wisely, as they will remain your seats throughout the year. I'm going to call the roll, and when I say your name, please identify yourself by raising your hand so I can enter your name in my seating chart. Now, first on my list is Gwendolyn Marie Albain. Thank you—do you prefer Gwendolyn or Gwen?"

I suffered through the better part of the alphabet trying to come up with ways I might subvert Miss Gaunt's plan to bind me to my current seat, far away from Josh and right next to Bob Berg. But I was so much in the middle, slightly toward the front, that a faked near-sightedness, far-sightedness, or deafness in one ear would be less than convincing. So when Miss Gaunt called my name, I knew all I could do was raise my hand.

"Timothy Thompson," Miss Gaunt said, already looking in my direction.

As I raised my hand, I heard from my left the voice of Bad Bob. "That's Tim Thompson, ma'am. He goes by 'Tim-Tom'."

I cast my eyes to Miss Gaunt's sweet, pruny face, which, in another micro-expression, briefly lost its pleasant smile in favor of a slight pursing of the lips. But she again chose to ignore Bad Bob and looked at me. "Do you prefer Timothy or Tim?"

"Timothy, Miss Gaunt." She and I were bonding.

After homeroom, Josh and I had a moment to compare schedules. I had been concentrating so hard on finding my homeroom that I had not so much as glanced at the rest of the schedule.

"Hey, we've got biology together third period," Josh said excitedly.

But I hardly even registered his presence, for my eye had frozen on the teacher's name listed under second period: Mr. Braun. Surely there were other physical education teachers at such a large high school—why did I have to get the Incredible Hulk?

Chapter 3
Alarm Bells

The shortened first period was social studies, which Mr. Leitner, a small, friendly man with a bad hairpiece, told us would "combine history, geography, politics, civics and"—get this!—"psychology to help you develop a more thorough understanding of this great country of ours." Except for my skepticism about psychology, born of years with Dr. Feelgood, the class sounded as if it just might be OK.

Then came the class I had been dreading since the end of homeroom: phy ed. Because of the shortened morning schedule on the first day, I was spared the humiliation of having to suit up for gym. (I am developmentally a year or so behind the other boys. Please don't make me go into details here.) Instead, we all sat on the gym floor cross-legged and in stocking feet—the stench!—and listened to Mr. Braun opine on the state of physical fitness in our nation today. As you might have guessed, he did not hold our generation in particularly high regard; in fact, the words *sissy* and *wuss* came up a number of times. While I do not preclude the possibility that it might have been due to paranoia, I felt sure that Mr. Braun was looking at me every time he intoned one of these words. The feeling was no doubt reinforced by Bad Bob Berg, who had sat himself directly behind me, prodding me in the spine with his big toe every time Mr. Braun said *sissy* (eight times) or *wuss* (five times).

The most extraordinary part of Mr. Braun's diatribe came at the end. I had just started to allow my mind to drift when Mr. Braun suddenly dropped his gym shorts to the floor and stepped out of them. He was now pacing in front of us in nothing but a jockstrap and T-shirt and talking about the importance of wearing "support for the family jewels." His family had apparently been quite wealthy, as his family jewels clearly needed a great deal of support. I found this whole display exceedingly embarrassing and began to stare at some point behind Mr. Braun but took note that he would "personally" do spot checks that we were wearing our athletic supporters. While I quickly added buying a jockstrap to my mental "To do" list, I shuddered inwardly as I considered what that "personal" inspection might involve. (To my knowledge, Mr. Braun never conducted a single spot check during my first months at Batshit High. Apparently he considered the threat enough to scare us all into compliance. It certainly worked with me.)

As we left the gym at the end of the period, we were all unusually quiet: what we had just witnessed could potentially scar us for life. Bad Bob broke the silence.

"I saw you watching Mr. Braun's ass, Tim-Tom," he taunted.

I knew myself well enough to realize that no clever retort was forthcoming, at least not in the next several minutes, so I didn't react to Bob's taunt.

"And how about them balls, huh?" my tormentor continued. "Pretty big, huh?"

"I didn't actually notice, Bob, but they seem to have made quite an impression on you," was my reply. I hadn't even thought about it, or I wouldn't have said it because I don't believe in any kind of teasing related to sexual orientation, however absurd or well-deserved. It did, however, serve the purpose of shutting Berg's horrid trap, and drew chuckles from the kind of boy I do not normally have on my side. I was well pleased, at least for the moment, even though the look on Berg's face was a warning of more—and worse—to come.

When I got to third period biology, Josh was already waiting for me at the door. "I heard about you and Berg," he said, beaming. Word traveled even faster here than at junior high.

"Which part?" I asked.

"Something about Mr. Braun's balls. What was *that* about?"

"Later, Josh," I said, for the teacher had just arrived, and I didn't want to get off on the wrong foot with her. Science was, after all, my best subject, which was why I was in AP biology rather than regular old general science, thus putting me and Josh in a class with mostly juniors and seniors.

"Biology," Mrs. Barker began, "is probably the most fascinating subject you will study all year. Why? Because it deals with the miracle of life! We will be looking at both the plant and animal kingdoms, and we will be discussing the different theories of how so many different life forms came into being."

Mrs. Barker's opening sentences were already setting off alarm bells inside my head. "The *miracle* of life"? "*Different* theories of how … different life forms *came into being*"? Admittedly, a word like *miracle* could be used in non-religious contexts, but how could there be *different* theories of species development—in a science classroom? I glanced around furtively. Josh was listening intently to Mrs. Barker's remarks, with no sign of apprehension. I noticed nothing on the faces of my other fellow students to indicate that they had heard anything untoward from our new teacher, so I concluded that I, as the son of Veronica Langley-Thompson, who had been described in the afore-mentioned magazine feature as "the Midwest's preeminent First Amendment attorney," was being overly sensitive.

Mrs. Barker continued. "In only a few weeks, we will start dissecting animals, at first simple organisms, followed by more and more complex creatures."

Two hands went up. One of them belonged to Megan Chow, a pretty Chinese girl I've had sort of a crush on since the middle of seventh grade. Megan was the only other freshman (freshwoman?) in the class besides me and Josh.

"Yes, young lady?" Mrs. Barker asked graciously. If she was annoyed that someone had interrupted her flow, she didn't show it.

"Do we have to dissect animals?" Megan asked. "If possible, I'd like to be excused from that."

"Well," Mrs. Barker smiled generously, "while I understand that some people might object to cutting into one of God's creatures, ..."

The alarm bells were now drowning out anything else Mrs. Barker might have said. "God"? In a public school? In a science classroom? I was outraged by the obvious illegality of this apparently casual name-dropping.

Now, please don't get me wrong. I believe in God. I even go to church fairly regularly, three out of four Sundays—more often, in fact, than either of my parents. (We have a very cool pastor who tells great stories. And he would be the first to admit that those stories are just that: stories.) But I also believe in the separation of church and state, and so should anyone who calls him- or herself an American.

So what did I do? Nothing. Call me a coward if you will, but I would like to think that my decision not to create a scene had more to do with tactics. At any rate, I chose not to say anything and quickly ruled out giving Mrs. Barker a heads-up after class that someone who cared about the First Amendment was listening. Instead I returned my thoughts to the classroom and registered that Mrs. Barker was not about to let Megan Chow or anyone else, vegetarian or otherwise, pass biology without desecrating a few animal carcasses, a decision which I, by the way, backed completely.

The rest of our first session with Mrs. Barker was uneventful, with lists passed out of equipment we would need to purchase throughout the semester, including approximate dates when each item would be required. This latter point was, in my view, extremely considerate toward those who might find it difficult to buy everything at once, but it also demonstrated a degree of advance planning I had yet to experience. Maybe this woman wouldn't be so bad after all, I thought, and determined to file away her religious references as minor indiscretions.

Josh and I had a minute at the end of the period to chat. "So, what did you think of our new science teacher?" I asked, trying not to betray my doubts.

"Nice," he said casually. "Ought to be good."

"Yeah," I replied. "Ought to be."

The rest of my first day at school was fairly routine and uneventful. Introductions were made, rules established, books handed out—the usual first-day-of-school stuff. That evening I went shopping with my dad to pick up some more things for school, including the jockstrap that was to protect me from a "personal inspection" by Coach Braun.

I'd have preferred the anonymous shopping mall that had recently been built just outside town, but Dad wanted to support the local merchants. Had we been going for a baseball mitt or similar implement, I'd have agreed with his show of civic support, but for something as intimate as a jockstrap, I really didn't want to go to Batshit Bob's Sporting Goods, where we were likely to run into various friends and acquaintances I'd rather not have imagining my scrawny frame in an athletic supporter.

As we entered Batshit Bob's ("We Put the Bat in Batshit"), it was Bob himself who greeted us.

"Hi, Paul. Long time, no see. Aren't you playing squash any more?"

"No, not since I pulled a hamstring a few years back."

"Yeah, none of us are gettin' any younger.—What can I do for you folks today?"

I started to say that we just wanted to look around, but my dad obviously didn't share my reservations about mention of my nether regions.

"Timothy here is starting high school, and he needs a jock."

I looked around. There wasn't anybody within earshot. My relief was short-lived, however. Instead of pointing us in the direction of men's intimate apparel, Bob accompanied us there.

"Well, son," he began, "you got any special needs down there?"

My inquiring glances were directed first at my dad, but he seemed to find the question normal. I looked back to Bob and croaked out an "I'm not sure what you mean."

"Well, first of all, is this just for gym class, or do you need a cup?"

I had no idea what he was talking about, so I answered that I merely wanted a standard athletic supporter for phy ed.

"And what kinda volume we talkin' here?"

"Volume?"

"You know: are you hung like a horse, or more like a toy poodle?"

I was already hatching an escape plan when Bob let out a laugh that I'd describe as a guffaw. Smiling from ear to ear, he said, "Don't worry, kid. I'm just joshin' ya. It's one-size-fits-all—just grab one in your waist size."

Only then did I realize that we were already standing in front of the item in question, and I picked one up.

"Is that it?" Bob asked. When I nodded, he walked with us to the cash register and gave me one of the free mini baseball bats the store was famous for. Normally they're only handed out at Batshit High football games—go figure—or given away with a purchase of $25 or more. In this case I think he saw it as compensation for the emotional trauma he had caused. If I never saw Batshit Bob again, I thought, it would be too soon.

Dad and I finished my school shopping without further incident. After all, things like pens and compasses bear little danger of embarrassment, although there was a moment when I thought the French curve I needed for my trigonometry class might lead to some discomfort. (Other boys in puberty will understand what I'm talking about.)

Chapter 4

The God Question

That Wednesday, we had our regular family dinner. It began as usual, with Mother greeting us and asking about our new-school experiences. Goth Girl, of course, had nothing to say, so I decided to dive in with the question that had been plaguing me since Mrs. Barker's class on the first day.

"Mom," I began, "what do we believe in?"

Both my parents were looking intently at me. Goth Girl pointed her head in my general direction, but her eyes, as per usual, were disconcertingly unfocused.

"Well, I can't really answer that question, Timothy, because I can only speak for myself. And it's rather a broad question. But I can give you an example: I believe in freedom of speech."

"And religion?" I wanted to know.

"Yes, of course. I believe in freedom of religion. Everyone should have the right to believe in whatever God they believe in," she said, glancing somewhat nervously at GG, "or don't believe in."

"And what do *you* believe in? Do you believe in God?"

All forks were down, all eyes focused on me, including GG's, for the first time in recent memory.

After a beat, my mother slowly gathered her words. "Well, Timothy, as you know, we're Unitarian."

GG was still staring at me, possibly in disbelief, but it was difficult to ascertain her emotions because she was careful never to allow them anywhere near her face.

Dad picked up where Mother had left off. "That's right, Buddy. We may not be the biggest church-goers, but we're solidly Unitarian."

I picked up my knife and fork and began to cut pensively at a piece of meatloaf. Goth Girl was the first to deflect her gaze, then my parents picked up their utensils and slowly began eating. Before the silence could reach deafening intensity, I made another attempt.

"I looked up Unitarianism on Wikipedia," I said. "It seems to cover a lot of ground. I mean, some Unitarians seem to believe in the whole works, others in nothing at all. Which is why I was wondering what *you* believe in. Mom? Dad?"

Once again, I sensed that I had GG's attention.

After pretending to swallow a bite of meatloaf and clearing his throat at great length, my dad gestured widely. "All this," he said, "is proof to me that God exists. And it isn't important to me what we call him, or her, or it. To me there's a Supreme Being out there, somewhere, and we're going to have to answer to that Being some day. So now you know."

My mother couldn't quite help but look surprised, though she tried to cover it with her napkin. All eyes were now on her; it was clearly her turn to take a position on the God question. She took a very large sip—more a gulp—of wine.

"For my part," she hedged, "things aren't quite so clear as they are for your father."

She wanted that statement to suffice and demonstratively tucked into the mashed potatoes to drive the point home. A tiny drop of gravy fell onto her sleeve, and she made a show of dabbing the spot with her napkin and water from her water goblet. (For some reason Dad had rolled out the good tableware to go with that night's somewhat basic meal.) I would have allowed her to get away with what was essentially a sound bite, but Dad was having none of that.

"Would you care to elaborate, Ronnie?" he asked. I found Dad's question quite brave, as it was already perfectly clear that Ronnie did not at all care to elaborate. Indeed Mother cast him a glance over her glasses that could have melted iron. Surprisingly, Dad stood his ground.

"Fine," she began, "I merely wanted to say that, although I don't actively *doubt* the existence of what your father has referred to as a 'Supreme Being,' I have yet to see any evidence of his or her existence. In life, as in the courtroom, I like to go on hard facts, and in the absence of those, I choose to reserve judgment."

"So what you're saying," my dad commented, "is that the jury is still out on the matter."

"Yes, something like that."

And with that, dinner conversation ceased for the evening. Dessert was not offered, although I know for a fact that Dad had made his chocolate mousse, everyone's favorite. (I have included his recipe in an addendum.) Our parents dismissed GG and me in the usual manner, but there was none of the usual post-Wednesday-dinner flirtation in the kitchen afterwards. I was fully expecting Wednesday night dinners to be canceled or at least to become a less regular feature of our lives under one roof, but these hopes have since been dashed. It seems that once my mother has set her mind on something, no setback small or large can dissuade her.

I should like to point out that terminating our quality time as a family had not been my purpose in initiating the theological discussion. Nonetheless I did note a certain elation when it seemed a distinct possibility. That evening Goth Girl even rewarded me with a punch in the left bicep and the longest utterance I had heard from her since her drift into whatever it was she was into: "Nice going, Slugger." No one had ever called me "Slugger" before, and to this day I am still not quite certain to what degree GG meant it as a term of endearment and to what extent it was ironic, since the words were spoken with no perceptible intonation.

For three full days after that fateful conversation, GG showed something like recognition when we crossed paths in the hall, so my dinner-time Q&A had been not only enlightening, but also somewhat beneficial.

Chapter 5

The Trouble Begins

School continued business as usual for the first week and a half. There was the customary extortion of lunch money, the taunts of Bob Berg and his friends, and the organized and officially sanctioned humiliation that was gym class. In fact, if the pranks of upper-classmen hadn't been added to the mix, I would have said that high school was not much different than junior high.

One thing that was all too familiar from junior high was the level in most of my classes. It was Low. As in really, really low. In those early days I didn't learn anything of an academic nature, although I was learning a great deal about the human condition: some people are simply not cut out to learn certain things, and it seemed almost cruel that society made them pretend to try. What purpose was served by teaching a future taxi-driver to calculate the area under a curve, an aspiring model the difference between a solution and a mixture, or a geek like me how to mount a pommel horse?

Actually, there was one class that was proving a challenge: German. I had chosen to learn the language of Einstein and Nietzsche rather than that of Pepé Le Pew or Speedy Gonzales, and I found for the first time in my life that I actually had to spend time on it outside the classroom. It wasn't like my perfect GPA was in danger or anything, but I was to that point unused to the concept of "studying." When I made the mistake of complaining to Josh, my best friend, that I was going to have to work to get an A in German, he showed no sympathy. In fact, he made a sarcastic remark, welcoming me to the world "the rest of us" live in. I have made a mental note never again to mention that I already know most of what passes as new at school, and that I acquire what little I have not yet read about simply by hearing it once.

Upon rereading that last paragraph, I realize that it may come across as terribly arrogant to anyone who has to struggle to keep up in school. In my defense I would like simply to say that it is not my fault that I have an IQ of 170 and come from a home where reading was always encouraged. Nor do I feel guilty about the fact that I am fortunate enough to possess total recall about anything I have ever seen or heard (or smelled, for that matter) since I was three.

You, dear Reader, might be wondering why I am not in a school for the gifted, or indeed why I am still at the normal grade level for my age. The answers to those questions are simple and complex at the same time.

My parents noticed my unusual intellect at a very early age and had me tested. I can remember that they agonized over the results for several weeks, the question being whether to send me to a school where my talents would receive special attention. They decided against the geek school for two reasons, and I respect my parents all the more for both of them. First of all, they didn't like the idea of sending me away and carrying on a vacations-only relationship with their beloved son. And secondly, they didn't feel it would be "right" to segregate children by their intellectual capacities. Both of them were strong believers in public education and would simply not have felt justified in taking their child out of the system for his—or their—personal gain.

And every time the question was raised whether I shouldn't skip a grade or three, my size was trotted out by the school psychologist as reason enough to hold me back. Apparently they feared that I would be ostracized by the other children for being younger and smaller than the rest of the class. So now I am only ostracized for being the know-it-all who skews the grading curve.

If popularity is the currency in high school, I am very poor indeed. No one likes a geek, other than other geeks, of course. I am, however, occasionally able to make points with my cohorts, for example when I involve the teacher in a discussion that, to them, seems to serve to delay the imparting of new material, or when I have to correct something the teacher has said. Not that I would ever do either of those things to make points with my classmates!

Making points was the farthest thing from my mind on that fateful Wednesday when I started all the trouble. I'd exchanged pleasantries with Miss Gaunt in homeroom, participated in an animated discussion of the relative merits of democracy and a "benevolent dictatorship" in Mr. Leitner's social studies class, and nearly died running laps in Mr. Braun's phy ed torture chamber—a normal day, in other words. And now it was time for biology with "Ma" Barker, as she had come to be known.

From the preparations that were going on, I could see that Mrs. Barker was planning to show us a film on the SmartBoard™. She was having the usual problems anyone over the age of 21 seems to have with all things technical. Of course no one was helping her, and she was too proud to ask for help. With amazing technical prowess I diagnosed the problem within milliseconds: Mrs. Barker had moved the laptop that was to stream the DVD a tad too far, and the cord was no longer inserted firmly in its socket. I briefly debated with myself whether to help her, but Beth Feinstein saved me from further agonizing—and the teacher from further embarrassment—by silently getting up and inserting the dangling cord properly.

To her credit, Mrs. Barker not only thanked Beth; she also admitted to her own inadequacies. "Thanks, Beth," she said. "I'm such a dunce when it comes to gadgets." This predictably drew a few chortles from the class of geeks—this was AP biology after all—and put us all in the mood for the multimedia lesson that was to follow.

The film started out harmless enough. Pretty nature pictures were followed by scientists talking about a meeting they had held in Pajaro Dunes, California, where they had together questioned long-held theories. Then I realized that the theory they were talking about was evolutionary theory. I saw where this was going, and I didn't much like it. My mother had regaled us with stories of various legal cases involving creationism and its stealth brother, intelligent design, and I knew that what Mrs. Barker was showing us was the secular equivalent of forbidden fruit.

As tantalizing as I found the prospect of hearing and viewing that which is so clearly *verboten*, I sprang into action. No, I didn't leap from my seat and demand that this outrage be stopped, although it might have been good fun and an interesting test for my classmates. Instead I discreetly reached for my cell phone—talk about *verboten*!—and sent a text message to my mother: "Biol tchr shwg intell dsgn mov! What 2 do?"

A minute later my mother texted back: "Nothing. I'll take care of it. Mom. PS: Pls use fwr abbrevs nxt tm!"

Then, at approximately the 11-minute mark, as the film's narrator was talking about "looking for alternative answers" to Darwinian theory, Principal Powers' voice could be heard coming from the PA system, which could also be used as a room-to-room intercom. "Mrs. Barker?" he called.

After pausing the film, Mrs. B. answered with a certain degree of apprehension, "Yes, Mr. Powers?"

"I understand you're showing a film to your AP biology class?"

"That's right."

"Because I've just had a fax from a local attorney demanding that you 'cease and desist' voluntarily or she'll have an injunction within the hour. Can you imagine what the problem might be?"

I am quite sure that Mrs. Barker not only imagined, but knew very well what the problem was. The fact that she—along with nearly everyone else in the room—was staring at me was proof enough for me that she was aware that showing this particular documentary in a public school was not altogether in alignment with the First Amendment to our nation's Constitution. Nonetheless her answer to Mr. Powers was an innocent, "I wouldn't know, Mr. Powers."

"Well then, why don't you put off showing this movie and bring it by my office during the break so we can talk about it?"

"Of course, Mr. Powers," she agreed, and he clicked off.

Mrs. Barker was facing away from the class as she drew a very deep breath, which I assumed was to muster strength for the inevitable attack on the student with the famous attorney mother. But this teacher was always good for a surprise, as I was to learn. She turned toward us with the sweetest of smiles and said, "Well, it seems we cannot continue with the lesson I had planned, but there's plenty of time left for a review of what we've done so far."

The inevitable groans quickly subsided when Mrs. Barker started dividing the class into teams and setting up a rather enjoyable competition which effectively refreshed our memories of all the concepts we'd discussed since the beginning of the school year—not much considering we were only a week and a half into the semester, but it was useful and fun at the same time. The hour passed without further incident, and I couldn't detect even the slightest trace of a sneer as I filed past her on the way out the door.

Josh, of course, was waiting for me at a safe distance from the biology room. "What was that about?" was his incredulous greeting.

"I can't imagine what you're referring to," I responded in my best imitation of Mrs. Barker's reaction to Mr. Powers' interruption.

"You know what I'm talking about, Timothy. Why did you sic your mother on Mrs. Barker?"

"Now why does everybody assume it was me? Or my mother for that matter?"

"Three guesses," was Josh's reply, followed by a stare-down.

I gave up. "All right. Josh, didn't you see where that movie was going?"

"An interesting discussion of evolutionary theory?"

"If you call a Sunday school lesson interesting, yeah."

"What do you mean?" Josh seemed genuinely puzzled.

"Look, we're gonna be late for class. I'll explain it over lunch, OK?"

"OK, I guess. See you at lunch then."

When I met Josh less than an hour later, he was hanging with some of our nerdy friends, AP material all of them. With the greatest of pleasure I noted that Megan Chow was there too.

"So, spill!" demanded Josh, and the others chimed in with various versions of "What's going on, dude?"

"Well," I began, "Mrs. Barker was showing a movie which was meant to push intelligent design—in a science class!"

Instead of the outrage I had expected at this revelation, I was greeted by empty looks and hanging jaws, most unflattering looks for anybody, but particularly for nerds—except of course for Stuart Schneider, who always has his mouth hanging open and makes me want to give him a heavy-duty rubber band every time I see him. Just as I was about to express my dismay that the five assembled members of the Batshit intelligentsia hadn't a clue what intelligent design was, Megan Chow spoke up.

"You're saying the flick had an agenda? To push ID?" I found it so quaint and sexy that Megan didn't talk about "movies" or use the more pretentious term "films," but referred to them as "flicks." I vowed then and there to make her my girlfriend by the end of the school year.

"Absolutely," I acknowledged, still wondering why the others weren't up in arms about Mrs. Barker's effrontery. The answer was swift to follow in the form of a staggering admission by my friend Josh.

"As much as I dislike admitting ignorance of any kind—I do have a reputation, such as it is, to keep up—could somebody please tell me what in the world intelligent design is supposed to be?"

"Yeah," Stuart Schneider said, followed by assent from Clementine Ward and Lamont Williams.

"Let's all get our lunches," I said. "I'll try and explain it then."

Chapter 6

Creationism, Intelligent Design And Evolution In A Nutshell—Well, In A Lunch Hour

You can tell a lot about people by the food they eat. As my friends and I settled in with our respective lunches, I saw, for example, that Josh had a simple sandwich, an apple, a candy bar and a small thermos of milk which he had brought from home in a Star Wars lunch box. It didn't seem to bother Josh that he was—with the exception of a few of the special needs kids—quite literally the only student who still carried a lunch box to school. "They're just jealous," he said of the boys teasing him, "because it's vintage." While I seriously doubted whether those boys cared that he was carrying a more-than-30-year-old lunch box much less knew what "vintage" meant, I found it oddly endearing that Josh truly believed this.

Clementine bought a salad from the salad bar, onto which she squeezed a few drops of lime—"Good grief! Not lemon!"—and sprinkled approximately four grains of salt. Clementine was the only girl I knew who readily admitted to anyone who asked, even to total strangers who didn't, that she was on a diet. Most people were too polite to ask the obvious, "Why?" For Clem, as her friends called her, stood a glorious five feet seven inches and weighed in at 110 pounds. (I'm fairly certain she does not have an eating disorder: her skin tone and complexion are always vibrant, and the girl is a sheer bundle of energy.) How her tiny frame managed to support two rather voluptuous breasts, I will never comprehend. I could see, though, that Clem was splurging today: there were three garbanzo beans on her salad, next to the sprouts, mushrooms, celery, tomato wedges and other non-caloric ingredients.

Stuart had treated himself to some variety of mystery meat and the heaviest looking mashed potatoes it has ever been my displeasure to see, both of which were topped with what the sign at the front of the cafeteria line had announced as "hearty 'beef' gravy." If the quotation marks around the word *beef* didn't put you off, surely the fact that this substance had the appearance and consistency of industrial sludge should have done so. But Stuart was forever fearless in his food choices, as was further witnessed by the small gray globes ("fresh garden peas") which accompanied his meat and potatoes, but first and foremost by the luminous pink mass ("fluffy cherry ambrosia"—who comes up with these names?) that filled his dessert dish. I hoped that Stuart could keep his mouth closed long enough to swallow his food today, as I didn't want to see any of this stuff oozing out of his gaping gob.

Lamont had brought his lunch in a paper bag, which he pulled from his backpack. Lamont's mother was a nutritionist, and it was clear that she had packed his lunch: every item had been chosen with the utmost care to balance the meal, and nearly every item had been cut at some odd angle to hone it to exact nutritional expectations. Seven eighths of a sandwich, six and a quarter carrot sticks, four and three quarter orange wedges and a slice of brownie precisely one and one eighth of an inch square. It was no surprise that Lamont not only was healthy, but he looked it too. I am sure very few people at Batshit High realized that this tall, handsome, athletic-looking, young African American man was in fact only 12 years old. Lamont's "awkward age" might have explained why he was always dropping things or stumbling over non-existent objects, but those of us who had known him since junior high knew that he was merely clumsy and anything but the athlete the casual observer took him to be.

Megan had brought the most interesting lunch. This was the first time I had eaten with her, and so I was fascinated by the procedure. She produced a red, silky bag with a drawstring, in which was contained an extremely colorful, hinged and latched wooden box. As she opened the latch with those delicate fingers of hers, I actually started to become excited. Once she had opened the lid, my Megan looked like a high priestess about to celebrate some cult ritual, which in this case consisted of removing eight tiny packages from the box and placing them most deliberately around the table space in front of her, closing the box and returning it to its silken bag, drawing the bag shut and placing it carefully inside her backpack. Some of the little packages were wrapped in leaves of some sort, while the others were wrapped in colorful paper reminiscent of the box in which they had come. Mysterious symbols marked each package and apparently told Megan what was inside or in which order she was to open these marvelous gifts. Lunch with Megan was a bit like Christmas, except that she neatly folded each bit of paper or leaf after eating its contents and made a tidy pile before wrapping all the papers and leaves in the last of the lot and slipped the final package gracefully into the back pocket of her jeans. Ah, poetry in motion!

And me? Well, today was one of Dad's days for volunteering at the homeless shelter, so he hadn't packed me a lunch but given me lunch money instead. Since I had managed to keep the money until the lunch hour without it being extorted, I was able to buy myself a bacon cheeseburger, curly fries and a vanilla shake—except for the salad actually some of the healthier choices on offer that day.

Between bites of our various lunches, we reconstructed what we knew of the three main theories of the origins of the species: evolution, creationism and intelligent design. Only the first of these, of course, earns the scientific label "theory," the other two being mythology and an attempt to subvert constitutional restrictions, respectively.

> *[Aside: The difference between the scientifically accepted definition of the word "theory" and the layperson's understanding of the word is the source of much confusion. In the sciences, a theory is the best, simplest, most logical explanation for phenomena observed and studied in nature, usually over many years. In everyday use a theory can be something I cook up in my head on the spur of the moment to explain something I happen to witness. I can reject that sort of theory just as quickly as I concocted it, and without regret: "It was only a theory," I'd say.]*

"OK," I began our little lunchtime session, biting into a curly fry, "can I assume we're all on the same page here as far as Darwin is concerned? I mean, we all accept the theory of evolution, right?"

"Of course," Megan answered.

"I have Darwin's picture on the wall above my bed," Clem said.

"*On the Origin of Species* is my bible," Lamont joked.

"No doubt about it," Stuart said, losing half a mouthful of masticated mystery meat.

Josh didn't say a word. All eyes turned to him.

"What?" Josh asked defensively. "OK, I believe. Just don't tell my mom—or my pastor."

"Right," I tried to sum up. "So we agree that all species evolved from a common source?"

"Yes," everyone asserted.

"And the different species evolved in response to environmental factors?"

"Yes."

"And," I came to the final article of faith, "natural selection determined which adaptations would survive and which were doomed to extinction?"

"Yes!" everyone proclaimed with the vigor of a religious revival, with Lamont adding, "And my great-great-great-great-grandfather was an ape." Guffaws followed.

"Good," I said, "then we can move on to creationism."

Josh jumped in before I could go on. "Let me get this one, Timothy. All those years of Bible school qualify me.—Ok, guys, here goes. This dude called God created everything in the universe, including all the species, in six days, then rested on the seventh. This all happened 6,000 years ago, give or take, and humans shared the earth with the dinosaurs until they killed them all off."

"That's it?" asked Clementine incredulously.

"Yep," Josh said, "that pretty much covers it."

Stuart sat there staring at Josh with his mouth hanging open, though it was not entirely clear to me whether that was his normal look or astonishment written in his face. "That's just dumb," he finally said.

"I don't think that's a fair assessment," Megan scolded. "That story was concocted centuries ago to help simpler souls understand their world."

"So nobody actually believes it today?" Stuart inquired, still looking more puzzled than usual.

"Ah, my naïve friend," Josh countered, "that's where you're wrong. Every Sunday I go to a whole church full of people who believe every word of that story—and a lot more bizarre stuff than that. They believe it is the word of God, written in the holy Bible."

"Hallelujah!" Lamont said.

"Now now," I said. "Let's not make fun of other people's religion. I wouldn't want anybody to make fun of mine either."

Megan looked straight at me. "So you do have one? A religion I mean?"

I fidgeted slightly before saying "Yes." Had I lost my sweet Megan before I'd even got her?

"Interesting," was her only remark, and I didn't know how to read it, which was, of course, maddening for someone like me.

Josh interrupted my moment of reflection. "So what about this intelligent design stuff, Timothy? You and Megan seem to be the only ones here who know anything about it."

"Well, I haven't really researched it," Megan said. "I just know what I've picked up in newspaper articles. Like when Christian fundamentalists try and sneak it into the curriculum. Timothy, you probably know more."

I reveled in the sound of my name from Megan's pouty lips, but only for a moment, as the lunch hour was slowly drawing to a close. "Well, I don't know *that* much—mostly what my mother has said at the dinner table. But as I understand it, when the courts decided that public schools couldn't teach the biblical version of creation, somebody came up with an alternative theory."

Megan scoffed. "Alternative? It's a wolf in sheep's clothing, is what it is!"

"Basically," I continued, "it's creationism dressed up in scientific-sounding terminology and with no mention of God."

"So where does the 'intelligent' part come in?" Lamont objected.

"As I said, the proponents of ID don't talk about God, but instead they say that all the 'scientific' evidence points to an 'intelligent designer'."

"So they've basically renamed God in Josh's cute little creation story?" Clementine demanded.

Megan and I looked at each other. She spoke first. "Well," she said, "I think so, but we really need to find out more."

"And we need to be prepared so we can stop Mrs. Barker from indoctrinating our fellow students."

Stuart closed his mouth for a moment, apparently thinking. "But why would anybody believe this intelligent design stuff?" he wondered. "I mean, all the evidence points to evolution." Then, almost as an afterthought, "Doesn't it?"

Before anybody could comment, the bell rang. Amidst the commotion as half the student body of Omar L. Batshit High School got up and headed toward their next lessons, I managed to suggest that we all find out what we could about ID and be ready to discuss it at lunch the next day.

Chapter 7

Irreducible Complexity

Batshit High School was abuzz that afternoon with rumors of what had happened in third period AP biology. The rumors varied greatly, but all had two elements in common: the names Mrs. Barker and a freshman by the name of Timothy Thompson. Several also contained reference to a movie.

In a majority of cases, the accuracy of the reports circulating ended there. The most harmless version had Mrs. Barker sending me to see Principal Powers for having watched a video during her biology lesson; my favorite involved the discovery by Mr. Powers that Mrs. Barker and I had appeared together in a pornographic film. I briefly considered encouraging the spread of that particular rumor, figuring it could only serve to enhance my reputation, but I was fairly sure that anyone who was familiar with me would know better. By the final bell of the school day, I was being approached by total strangers who either congratulated or castigated me for getting Mrs. Barker fired.

It had not been my intention to have anyone fired, so I was appalled at the suggestion that I had done so. I even considered contacting my mother about representing Mrs. Barker in a wrongful dismissal suit against the school district but decided that could wait until I had confirmation of her actual firing. What I got instead was very different indeed.

Stuck to my locker was a note. This conjured up images of other notes that had been left for me: not-so-gentle teasing about my perceived sexuality, misspelled diatribes about something or other I had said in class, or threats of extended torture and slow death if I didn't deliberately take a dive on a test. The fact that this particular note was on flowery paper that said "God Is Love" at the top, next to which someone had written my name in similarly flowery letters, led me to believe—mistakenly—that this note did not contain anything threatening.

I opened the missive, and my eyes were immediately drawn to the signature, "Mrs. Barker." I had always thought that the phrase "my heart skipped a beat" was merely an expression, but at that moment I learned there was more to it than that. I actually felt a brief cessation of my cardiovascular functions, accompanied by a momentary vision loss and a sensation of nausea.

The tone of the note was friendly enough. All it said was, "Dear Timothy, If you have a chance, please drop by my room after school. Thank you, Mrs. Barker." Pretty harmless stuff, really, but I felt certain there was a threat veiled somewhere within the seemingly innocent text. At the very least, this "invitation" would lead to an ugly confrontation; at worst, Mrs. Barker would be waiting behind the door with an axe.

I was deliberating my options. I could go to face my fate like the man I wasn't (but so desperately wanted to be), or I could wait until tomorrow's class for the inevitable dressing down. At least with the second option there would be witnesses, I told myself, but even as I pondered, my legs were propelling me toward the biology room—involuntarily, as it were. Another peculiar phenomenon was the music. The after-school hustle and bustle was slowly being drowned out by the sound of music. It took me a moment to realize what was happening: the real, external sounds of students shouting, slamming locker doors and shuffling toward the exits were in decrescendo, while an internal soundtrack was in crescendo. It took yet another moment before I recognized the music playing inside my head. It was the theme song from the spaghetti western *The Good, the Bad and the Ugly*, a film which features in my parents' DVD collection.

The score my brain had chosen for the next and perhaps final scene of my life seemed highly appropriate, but which of us—Mrs. Barker or I—was to be the Clint Eastwood character, riding off in the end with the gold? And which of us was Angel Eyes and would end up in the unmarked grave? The theme reached its climax just as I reached the door of Mrs. Barker's room and came to a sudden end as I knocked and entered.

Mrs. Barker was not wielding an axe or any other implement which might be used to bring about my premature demise. Instead she wore a friendly smile and greeted me with the words, "Ah, Timothy, I'm glad you could make it." Mrs. Barker was either a tremendous actor, unnaturally forgiving or still gainfully employed.

I mustered all my courage and vowed not to allow my voice to break when I spoke. In this I failed miserably. "Yes, ... erm ... Mrs. Barker. You ... erm ... wanted to ... erm ... talk to me?"

"Yes, Timothy. I had a little chat this afternoon with Mr. Powers. But of course you know that."

"Yes, Mrs. Barker. Erm ... I ... I just want you to know ... erm ... that I didn't want you to ... erm ... be fired."

"Fired?" said Mrs. Barker, incredulous. "No, no, nothing of the kind. Mr. Powers was merely concerned that the movie I was showing you might not be—how shall I put this?—appropriate in the context. And that was obviously your concern as well, I assume."

At least I wouldn't have to confess that I was the one who had called in the cavalry. She obviously knew. "Yes, Mrs. Barker," I croaked.

"Well, there will be no more open exchange of ideas in my science classes, I'm sorry to say," Mrs. Barker said wistfully.

"Open exchange of ideas?"

"Yes, Timothy. You see, I'm a great believer in teaching the controversy and letting your young minds decide which of the legitimate, conflicting theories about life and the species is the correct one. But it seems that the courts are terribly dogmatic that way. They only accept one theory, Darwinism, as true and won't allow intelligent design, which has at least as much going for it, to be presented."

"When you say 'teaching the controversy,' what exactly do you mean?" I asked, having got my voice back.

"The whole debate about Darwinian theory as opposed to intelligent design, of course. I think it's a real shame we can't discuss it in the classroom." She drew a deep breath and sighed. "But that's the way it is. Anyway, I just wanted to let you know that there are no hard feelings. We'll see each other in class tomorrow."

Once again, this had not been the reaction I'd been expecting and dreading. Mrs. Barker had class, I decided, said my good-byes and headed home. Tonight was family night, after all, and attendance was required.

When I got home, Dad was in the kitchen getting supper ready, Goth Girl was in her room, as evidenced by the chants seeping through the floorboards from her room, and Mother hadn't arrived home yet.

"Hey, buddy," Dad said when I followed the scent of roasting meat into his realm. "How was school?"

I tried the sauce that was stewing on the stovetop to cover for my hesitation to answer this simplest of questions. Licking my chops, I finally said, "OK, I guess. Interesting." Then, "When's dinner?"

"It'll be another hour, Timmy. Your mom's secretary called and said she was running late. Something about a school board matter."

I don't think Dad saw my face go pale, but I excused myself and went up to my room as quickly as possible, ostensibly to do my homework. But the research I needed to do had not been assigned. I wanted to see if I could find the movie Mrs. Barker had started showing us and finish watching it.

Sure enough, it was available at full length online for free. I fast-forwarded to the point where Mr. Powers had interrupted our viewing and watched it diligently. What I saw shook my beliefs to their very core. A biochemist, a philosopher of science and even an evolutionary biologist were openly questioning the theory of evolution. And they had what seemed to me rather strong arguments, including a principle I had never heard of, something called "irreducible complexity."

Why, I wondered, had my science teachers and all the scientific literature I had read up to now ignored this tantalizing argument against evolution? Irreducible complexity basically means that some part of an organism is too complex to have evolved bit by bit over time. The film used the example of a bacterium which has a sort of rotary motor, known as the flagellum, that enables it to swim. This motor is highly complex and can only function, the theory has it, if every single part of it is present. How then, these scientists argue, can the flagellum have evolved, since evolution is a gradual process? If only a single part of the motor appeared as a mutation, it wouldn't have had any function and so wouldn't have survived the evolutionary process while waiting for the next parts of the motor to come along. This, the ID theorists argue, blows a huge hole in Darwin's theories. The only feasible explanation, according to intelligent design proponents, is that an intelligent designer must have constructed the flagellum motor.

After watching the movie, I frankly didn't know what to think, and it was in this state of vulnerability that I found myself when Mother called Goth Girl and me down to dinner.

Mother was supercharged, a veritable mama grizzly. "I want to thank you for drawing that woman to my attention, Timothy, that Mrs. Barker. I guess we shut her up."

"Yes, we did, Mother," I replied.

And of course Dad wanted to know what we were talking about, so Mother filled him in, with me unenthusiastically adding details from the classroom that she could not know.

Mother continued by saying that she had put everything else on hold for the rest of the day, using the time to prepare a brief—"just in case"—and a petition for the school board to have Mrs. Barker removed from her post.

"Wait, Mom, don't," I said.

Goth Girl, who to this point had said nothing and barely moved a muscle that was not necessary to the intake of calories, turned her head toward me and focused her eyes on my face. I was not quite clear whether my contradiction or GG's sudden sign of consciousness startled my parents more.

"What do you mean, 'wait,' Timothy?" my mother asked.

"Yeah, buddy, I would have thought you'd be pleased," Dad added.

I felt terribly conflicted. On the one hand, of course I was pleased that Mother had been so interested in my case that she had spent a good part of her day working to support me. On the other hand, Mrs. Barker had been so ... gracious about the whole thing that I didn't want to see her get the boot. And now this whole irreducible complexity thing! I no longer knew what to believe.

Finally I spoke. "Mother, I think it's great what you did. I'm just not sure I want to take it any further."

"OK," Mother said hesitantly. "I wouldn't want to embarrass you, Timothy. But would you mind telling me why you don't want to take the matter any further?"

"Well, Mrs. Barker asked me to come to her room after school, and …"

"Did she threaten you in any way?" Mother asked.

"No, no, nothing like that," I said. "In fact, she was very nice about the whole thing. She just thinks it's a pity that she can't teach the controversy and let us decide. And I kind of agree."

"Did she put it like that, Timothy?" my dad asked. "'Teach the controversy'?"

"Yes," I answered. "Why?"

My parents looked at each other knowingly. My mother spoke. "'Teach the controversy' isn't just your teacher talking, Timothy. It's a slogan that ID propagandists have coined to suggest that there *is* a controversy in the scientific community, when in fact no serious scientist supports such stuff and nonsense." (My mother is similarly enamored of alliteration as I am.)

"But I just watched the movie that Mrs. Barker was trying to show us. There were real scientists in it, and they were talking about a concept called irreducible complexity that really got me thinking. Maybe this intelligent design theory is right."

"Tim-boy," my dad began, "listen. I'm proud of you for wanting to check into this. It says a lot about you and your sense of fairness. But you need to apply that super-brain of yours to some critical thinking: Who are the so-called scientists in this movie? What are their credentials? Who's paying them? What do their peers have to say about their theories? I'm no expert on either evolution or intelligent design, but from everything I've heard from sources I trust, ID is a bunch of hooey."

When my dad used the word *hooey*, I thought I caught the trace of a smile on GG's face, but it was hard to tell for sure. I'd lost her attention at the words "irreducible complexity," and she was no longer looking in my direction, her head turned instead toward the plate of pot roast the rest of us weren't doing justice.

We fell silent for a few minutes, but then I had to ask, "Mom? If ID is, as Dad says, nothing but hooey, what's wrong with teaching it alongside evolution and letting students figure it out for themselves?"

"The First Amendment," Mother answered immediately, though the words were garbled slightly by a mouthful of Dad's potatoes dauphinoise. (I am also attaching this recipe in an addendum.) My mother never talked with her mouth full, but the First Amendment was even more important to her than matters of decorum. She finished chewing and dabbed at her mouth with her napkin.

"The First Amendment is what's wrong with teaching ID in public schools. The courts have decided that intelligent design is religiously motivated and has nothing to do with science. If we allow it to be taught in the science classroom, we're giving it a legitimacy it doesn't deserve."

"Look at it this way, son," Dad said. "How would you feel about it if your biology teacher were to get up and tell you that God created the heavens and the earth and all the creatures in it?"

"I'd say that's religion—something that belongs in church, not in school."

"Well, that's exactly what ID is. Sure, they don't talk about God, but it's the same story. They just substitute 'intelligent designer' for the word 'God'."

"OK, I know we're not supposed to allow religion in school because the Constitution says so," I objected, "but what's the harm if we do?"

As soon as I said this I regretted it, as I fully expected Mother to explode. The notion that her own flesh and blood would question the wisdom of her precious First Amendment at her dining-room table was pretty audacious, after all. The reaction I got was not at all what I'd expected.

Mother looked very thoughtful as she put her knife and fork down on her plate. "That's a very good and important question, Timothy," she said. "After all, some of the first European immigrants to this continent were highly religious people."

"The Pilgrims?" I ventured.

"That's right, the Pilgrims," Mother confirmed. A gold star for Timothy. "And slightly later the Puritans. As we were all taught in school they came in search of religious freedom and tolerance. But the fact of the matter was, they only wanted religious freedom and tolerance for themselves. They didn't exactly practice it with anybody else."

"I didn't know that." I felt humbled.

"They don't like teaching these things in school—the myths are so much nicer," Mother continued. "No, the Pilgrims were not a tolerant people. They didn't want anybody in their colony who didn't adhere to their own brand of Christianity. The Puritans banished dissenters from the colony, didn't allow Catholics in, and they even hanged a couple of Quakers along the way. And that's just the Christians! I haven't even mentioned the people they thought were witches." She glanced nervously in Goth Girl's direction, but no reaction was forthcoming from that quarter.

"After independence, there were states that didn't allow Jews to hold public office. And since then the country has taken in untold numbers of Muslims, Hindus and probably others I can't think of right now. So when you talk about letting religion into the public schools, the question is: whose religion? Whose creation story are you going to teach? And what have any of those stories got to do with science? So with what justification do people want them in the science classroom?"

Wow. A lesson in history, law and ethics all rolled into one—in the course of just a few minutes! My mom is pretty awesome sometimes.

"Hmm," I said, munching on some green beans. "So what does it take to convince people? I mean, a lot of people seem to believe in creationism. Josh said everybody in his church believes. And I just saw a poll online that said about 40% of Americans accept the creation story as true."

My dad answered this time. "I doubt they really all believe in creationism, Timmy. They're just afraid to say what they really think. Peer pressure and all."

"I thought only kids had to deal with peer pressure."

"No, son, only the context changes," Dad said, somewhat ominously. I would pursue that subject at a later date. Right now I had other priorities.

"So how do I convince Mrs. Barker she's wrong?"

Mom and Dad looked at each other knowingly, in that annoying way adults have when they think we're being naïve. "The truth of the matter is," Dad said, "you probably can't."

"But she's a teacher," I argued. "I'm sure she'll listen to reason." I still had lots of work to do to find the evidence I was going to need to counter ID and this irreducible complexity thing, but—ironically—I was taking it on faith that science had the answers.

"Exactly, Timothy," Mother said. "She's a teacher—a science teacher no less. I'm sure she's seen all the evidence, but she's chosen not to believe it."

"But that doesn't make sense," I said—not so terribly confidently.

Chapter 8
A Challenge

When I went to school the morning after the movie incident, I felt super-charged. I knew I had my work cut out for me—after all, proving that evolution is true to an already scientifically educated teacher was no mean task—but I was still determined to make it happen. The family dinner, which had had three active participants in a real conversation, only served to boost my resolve.

Miss Gaunt was still at the school, and she took me aside after homeroom. "Be careful, young Timothy," she said in an ominous whisper. But before I could ask her what exactly she was warning me about, she dashed off, saying only that she didn't want to be late for her first-period drafting class.

My sense of foreboding intensified during my own first period, when Mr. Leitner without explanation changed topics in our social studies lesson from "forms of government" to "the First Amendment in theory and practice" with particular attention to separation of church and state. I did not need a little birdie to tell me that the teachers had a news network that matched in efficiency and speed that of the students, or possibly even surpassed it.

As fascinating as I always found discussion of our nation's Constitution, it was difficult for me to concentrate, as my mind was largely on third-period biology and what might possibly be awaiting me there. For the first time I found myself actually thinking ahead with pleasure to phy ed with Mr. Braun. At least there I would not have to deal with the issues that, I sensed, were going to define my stay at Batshit High. I would find out soon enough how wrong I was.

I managed to get suited up without anyone taking notice of me, and I headed into the gymnasium with the other boys. Unlike other days when we had phy ed, Mr. Braun was not waiting impatiently for us at center court. We could see him through the window of his office, which overlooked the gym. He was on the phone and looked angry, which we all assumed was not a good thing. I wondered whether there was a mathematical formula with which I could calculate how many laps we would have to run in order to work off Mr. Braun's frustrations.

It didn't take long for Coach to lumber toward our frightened little group. Even the bigger brutes and the better jocks were cowering by the time Mr. Braun reached us, his whistle clenched between his teeth. "Where's Thompson?" he shouted with a scowl.

I identified myself with a timid raising of my left hand. "Here, sir."

"Good," he said. "You're captain of Team A. Berg, you're in charge of Team B. Choose your men."

Although I somehow sensed that it was folly to speak up, at the same time my left brain was begging me for the information required to choose the best team. "What's the game, Coach?" I asked.

"Whatever game I damn well decide to make it!" was the less than informative answer. Berg and I began choosing our teams, both favoring bulk over speed. As usual, the scrawniest boys were left for the end, the only difference today being that I wasn't one of them. For the briefest of moments, I felt grateful toward Coach Braun and somewhat empowered.

"OK, girls," Mr. Braun began, "the game is dodgeball." Then, upon hearing the groans, "Now stop your whining! I want you to get six balls out of the bin over there. Your team gets one point for each boy on the opposing team you hit, and ten points for hitting the captain. Anybody who gets hit is eliminated, except for the captain, who stays in till the very end. The first team to make 150 points can hit the showers, the other team runs laps till the end of the hour.—Any questions?—I didn't think so. Now go to it!"

I went to biology severely welted and exhausted from running laps. Josh met me outside the classroom. "What happened to you?" he demanded, nodding toward the large, raised red patch on my right cheek.

"A little present from Mr. Braun," I told him.

"He hit you?"

"Not exactly," I said. "Hey, we'd better get inside before the bell rings. I don't want to give Mrs. Barker an excuse to throw something at me."

And throw something at me she did: humility, kindness and guile.

Once we had all settled into our seats and some students had got over their surprise at Mrs. Barker's presence (for the rumor that she had been fired had persisted throughout the morning), she began the lesson. "First of all, I'd like to apologize to everyone for my mistake yesterday."

We were all a bit puzzled by this opening statement and looked around to see how our classmates were reacting. Mrs. Barker continued.

"Not realizing that the contents of the little movie I started showing was—how shall I put this?—inappropriate for the classroom, I tried to show you something I happen to believe would stimulate discussion. But apparently the laws of the land are such that all discussion or even mention of certain scientific theories is prohibited.

"Again, I am truly sorry that, in my zeal to promote the free airing of ideas, I so clearly violated court decisions. In particular I'd like to extend my sincere apology to Timothy, who was more aware of legal precedent than I was and put a stop to my error before any harm was done."

As she looked at me, she saw the large welt on my cheek. Approaching me, she showed (or feigned) concern, "Oh, dear. What happened to you, Timothy?"

"Nothing, Mrs. Barker," I lied. The sting was almost unbearable. "Just a stray ball in phy ed."

"Well, if you need to see the school nurse, you certainly have my permission."

"Thank you, Mrs. Barker," I said as cheerily as I could manage. "I'll be fine."

"Very well then, let's move on to our first look at one-celled creatures. By the way, the list of supplies that I gave you all on the first day? Well, I've had to make some adjustments to my lesson plan for this year, and you'll be needing everything two weeks earlier than it says on the list. We start dissecting a week from Monday."

There were a few muffled groans, and I could detect several pairs of eyes glaring at me, even though I diverted my own to study my desktop. More disturbing to me was the sudden change in lesson plan. Did this mean we would be skipping over the origin of species? I didn't see how a biology course could get by without mentioning Darwin or the theory of evolution, so I assumed that that rather central concept of biology would be dealt with at a later date. As Mrs. Barker launched into the structure of the living cell, I had to marvel at her performance. She had, on the one hand, demonstrated true grace and poise in her apology, even thanking the person who had shut down her ID propaganda operation, or as she framed it, her free airing of ideas.

On the other hand, she had managed to achieve any number of farther-reaching goals. She had awakened the curiosity of those students who hadn't already wondered what it was that she had been trying to show the class the day before. I had no doubt that quite a few of them would be online searching for that which was so subversive that "all discussion or even mention" of it was prohibited.

Mrs. Barker had also managed to reveal beyond a doubt that I was indeed the one who had prevented the class from partaking of this apparently juiciest of forbidden fruits. And at the same time Mrs. Barker had established that she was not angry at me and could not be held responsible for the beating I had taken in the gym only minutes before, or those that were, I was certain, still to follow.

Yes, somehow I had become the villain, the one everyone loves to hate. And then there was the implicit challenge in our biology teacher's words. She was letting me and the others know that she was up for a debate. She felt confident enough in her alternative "scientific theory" that she was willing to have a "free airing of ideas." She had, after all, only wanted to "stimulate discussion." What, I knew everyone was wondering, could possibly be wrong with that? And despite my mother's reasoning, I too had my doubts that there was anything wrong with taking up the gauntlet Mrs. Barker had thrown down.

Yes, Mrs. Barker was definitely a class act, in every sense of the word.

Chapter 9

Know Thine Enemy

Lunch that day found the same group at my table as the day before. Megan, Josh and I filled in the others as to what had happened in Mrs. Barker's class that morning. Then came the inevitable question about my cheek, which was still pretty red, though not as swollen as it had been.

"Well, it seems Coach Braun doesn't like me much," I offered.

Stuart's jaw dropped a few millimeters from its already very open position. "Coach Braun hit you?" he exclaimed.

"No, he just invented a new kind of dodgeball, especially for me."

"But why?" Clementine wanted to know. "Do you think it has anything to do with the incident in Mrs. Barker's class?"

Although I had my suspicions, I held back. "I don't really know. I doubt it. But he did get a phone call at the beginning of the period that got him really worked up."

"I'll bet it was Mrs. Barker," Lamont said. "All sweet and 'Christian' to your face, but she can't wait to stab you in the back."

But Megan had her doubts. "I don't know, guys. Her apology sounded genuine before. And until we have proof, I don't think we should be accusing her."

I agreed with Megan—then again, I'd have agreed with Megan if she'd said the earth was flat and pigs could fly—and conversation moved on to what we'd found out about intelligent design. It turned out that we'd all stumbled over the same thing: irreducible complexity. We decided to ask our science guru, Mr. Grass, who also happened to be the faculty advisor to the Science Club.

The club met every Thursday after school, and on this particular Thursday attendance was higher even than at the sign-up meeting the week before. Mr. Grass was looking particularly dapper in his period costume (Guglielmo Marconi?), and he seemed blissfully unaware of the minor scandal that had gone on in the classroom just a few doors away from his own, where a lowly freshman had prevented a teacher from showing a movie by threatening legal action. We filled him in as best we could, then got to the problem that was bothering us.

"Mr. Grass, can you explain the concept of irreducible complexity for us," Megan asked, "and maybe tell us what's wrong with it?"

"Smoke and mirrors" was his cryptic reply.

When we all simply stared at him with puzzled looks, Mr. Grass explained. "Smoke and mirrors—the instruments of every good illusionist-magician. Irreducible complexity is nothing other than a distraction."

"It sounded pretty convincing to me," I confessed.

"Could you guys maybe clue the rest of us in?" this junior called Cliff Jablonski pleaded. "Judging from the looks on the faces around me, I'm not the only one who doesn't have the slightest idea what you're talking about."

Mr. Grass immediately went into teaching mode, adjusting his wing collar with chalky hands and leaping up from his chair. He pulled down a familiar chart, the one that shows how humankind evolved from lesser apes. "I'm sure you've all seen this at one time or another? This chart shows how, over millions of years, modern man came into being."

"And woman," Clem interjected.

"And woman," Mr. Grass conceded. "The chart is based on scientific evidence and goes back to Darwinian theory from the 19th Century."

He looked around the room to check that we were following. "Evolution is generally accepted as fact throughout the scientific community. Recently—and I mean in the last forty years or so—a group of skeptics has emerged, people who call themselves scientists, who are trying to poke holes in evolutionary theory.

"They basically say that random mutation cannot explain every change that takes place within a species, and that it certainly can't explain transitions from one species to another."

Mr. Grass paused again to allow this to sink in. I could see the questions forming in the heads of my fellow science fans. Again, it was Cliff Jablonski who formulated the one that was foremost on everyone's minds.

"So how *do* they explain the existence of different species? If it weren't for evolution, all there'd be is one-celled organisms."

"Ah, I'm glad you asked that question, Cliff," Mr. Grass said. "Well, these so-called scientists don't believe in common ancestry—that we all came from the first primitive organisms swimming about in the primordial swamp. They believe that each and every species was designed individually and came onto earth fully developed."

This was heresy—ah, the irony—to the science-minded crowd Mr. Grass was playing to, and those who were hearing it for the first time were suitably outraged. It occurred to me that Galileo had faced similar opposition when he first proposed that the earth revolved around the sun, and it made me wonder whether the scientists Mr. Grass was talking about so disparagingly might not be the new Galileos. Maybe they were the vanguard of scientific thinking, I wondered, and the vast majority of scientists were simply unwilling to discuss these radical new ideas solely on the grounds that they did not fit into established doctrine.

Mr. Grass quickly helped me to divorce myself from such doubts.

"Now, I'm very glad to see that you've all drunk the Kool-Aid™. But *why* do we believe in evolution?"

Hands went up as if we were in class and not a club. Mr. Grass called on Lamont.

"Because of the fossil record," Lamont offered.

"And observation of evolution in action—with viruses, for example," Megan added.

"Excellent," Mr. Grass said. "We base our conclusions on evidence. But what happens when we find something that our theories can't explain? What do we do then?"

The concept that we might not be able to explain everything scientifically seemed foreign to most of those present, so I jumped in. "We keep looking," I said simply.

"Exactly. We keep looking. In the past people filled in the gaps in our knowledge with gods. Where did fire come from? Easy: Prometheus stole it from the gods. What about thunder? That's Thor wielding his hammer. Having trouble accepting evolution? Invoke an 'intelligent designer'.

"They say that nature abhors a vacuum. Well, the human mind abhors gaps at least as much. So when there's a gap in our knowledge, there's always somebody quick to supply an easy answer, and more often than not, that answer is God. We call that 'God of the gaps argumentation'."

"So are you saying that irreducible complexity is the answer to a gap in evolutionary theory?" I asked.

"No, that's not what I'm saying at all. I'll get to irreducible complexity in a minute. The only gaps in the theory of evolution are small. They don't require a new theory at all. They only require a bit more research, a bit more observation. We need to keep looking.

"But instead, some people use the gaps to claim that evolution is a 'theory in crisis,' as they put it. It's not. No serious scientist I know of has ever said, 'Gee, evolution is falling apart. We'd better come up with something new.' No way. But that's what this group of pseudo-scientists we're talking about are saying."

"So they came up with intelligent design?" Stuart speculated.

"That's right," Mr. Grass confirmed. "They decided one day that they didn't like the theory of evolution, so they concocted this ridiculous notion—I'm not going to flatter ID by calling it a theory or even a hypothesis because there's nothing scientific about it—this idea that an intelligent designer had created all the species separately.

"And 'irreducible complexity'—this thing you're so worried about," he said, looking at Megan and me, "it's just something they added on later to give their wacky idea the appearance of legitimacy."

"So what is it?" Josh was getting frustrated. "How do these wackos define irreducible complexity?"

"OK, basically what they're saying is: life is too complicated to have happened by accident. They like to use the bacterial flagellum as their Exhibit A. Certain bacteria have this little tail-like thing that they use to move. They claim that the flagellum consists of distinct parts, just like an engine. If you take away any of those parts, the engine can't work."

Mr. Grass looked around. He was clearly enjoying having the rapt attention of an audience that was there voluntarily. He continued.

"So, if evolution happens piece by piece, how did something as complex as the flagellum motor come about? If a mutation put two parts together that didn't do anything, they wouldn't have survived natural selection. At least that's what the ID people say. So, what are the flaws in their argument so far?"

I found myself hoping that Mr. Grass's question was merely rhetorical, but the length of his pause suggested otherwise.

"Think, people," Mr. Grass said, gesticulating wildly enough to untuck his shirt. "You need to know what you're up against if you want to discredit these people. What are the flaws in their argument?"

"Well," I began sheepishly, "I guess I'd wonder what they mean when they talk about the 'parts' of the flagellum. I found this diagram online that looked like a technical drawing of an engine, crankshaft and all. I find it a little hard to believe that nature produced anything like that."

"Very good," Mr. Grass said, and he wrote "Definition of 'part' vague" on the board. "Anything else?"

Stuart was the next one to hazard a guess. "Is it true that natural selection wipes out any mutation that doesn't do anything? I mean, we still have an appendix, and it doesn't do anything except cause appendicitis."

"A good point, Stuart," Mr. Grass commended my gape-mouthed friend. "But your example isn't going to get you very far. You see, we're not sure that the appendix doesn't in fact have a function. But your basic idea is correct. There are lots of examples of useless things that still hang around although they serve no real purpose." He wrote "Uselessness ≠ elimination" on the board.

"In fact," he said with no small delight, "the flagellum itself is *not* irreducible in its complexity. I'm not sure of the exact number, but the flagellum of the *E. coli* bacterium consists of something like 500 different amino acids, and a Japanese scientist by the name of Kuwajima managed to cut out a third of them without reducing its function in the slightest! Now why, I ask, would an 'intelligent' designer create something that has so many superfluous parts? He wouldn't!

"And what's more, different bacteria have flagella with different compositions even though they do exactly the same thing. Again, why would an 'intelligent' designer come up with radically different, highly elaborate designs to do one and the same thing? Again, the answer is: he wouldn't!"

Mr. Grass looked well pleased with himself as everyone in the room nodded with conviction. But that wasn't all our Science Club advisor had to say on the subject—he obviously felt quite passionate about it. A brief image of a science department meeting which would inevitably include both him and Mrs. Barker flashed through my mind as he continued. I had to suppress a smile.

"Now some of you may have noticed that we have virtually ruled out the existence of an intelligent designer. But we haven't actually proved that evolution can lead to big changes. The skeptics would have it that individual species can adapt and evolve, but that those changes are small and don't explain the huge leaps that are necessary to account for the development of new species. Wrong!

"First of all, small changes add up. Even if only every tenth generation produced a change, over millions of years that's a lot of changes. And together those little changes make for some pretty big changes, and we have to start talking about new and different species.

"And secondly, this is what we call in logic an argument of incredulity. Basically what these people are saying is that they cannot imagine something like that happening, so it mustn't be true."

"Kind of like Thor's hammer and thunder," I interjected.

"No, Timothy," Mr. Grass corrected, "*exactly* like Thor's hammer and thunder. If I can't find an explanation for something, or I find an explanation too complicated, I just insert God into the equation and decide that that answers everything. Well, that might make me feel better, but it's not an answer—it's intellectual laziness, is what it is!"

"But Mr. Grass, we can hardly tell Mrs. Barker she's intellectually lazy," I objected.

He chortled and said, "No, I wouldn't really recommend it. But from what you told me before, I don't think she'll be talking about her beliefs in school any more."

Chapter 10
Quiet Before The Storm

The next week was fairly quiet at Batshit High. Rumor had it that I was somehow a force to contend with, so the bullies were leaving me alone for a while. The trouncing I had taken in Mr. Braun's gym class had also apparently satisfied his thirst for blood, which made the two or three gym periods a week bearable, though not, of course, enjoyable.

Even Mrs. Barker's biology lessons went off without incident, despite the fact that we had skipped over evolution. I listened intently but found no evidence that she was sneaking in any rarefied religious references.

Since "the incident," as my friends and I came to refer to Mrs. Barker's attempt to smuggle ID into the classroom, we had tried to establish contact with students who had Mrs. Barker in other periods, but to little avail. Nerds like us are not particularly skilled at networking, it seems.

I had a source in her first-period general science class, but Mike Petersson was, frankly, so dim that I doubt he'd recognize a creationist story if Mrs. Barker hit him over the head with Adam's rib while telling it. Mike, who was two years older than me and had grown up in my neighborhood, assured me that Mrs. Barker was teaching nothing but pure science. And he professed to be an expert on the subject since this was the third time he was doing 9th grade general science. Mike was proud of the fact that he was the only ninth-grader on the football team's first string—for the second year running. (Apparently it is not difficult to circumvent the GPA requirements for participation in extracurricular activities if you're into sports and have someone as influential as Coach Braun on your side.)

Mike and I were never really close. There was, of course, the age difference, and our interests diverged rather drastically: I was always the computer geek, he the burly jock. Still, we'd always been friendly, and I never had problems with bullies in the neighborhood after Mike put out word that I was under his protection. How I wished for a similar shield at school, but alas, Mike's and my paths rarely crossed here in academia. So what came next was a pleasant surprise.

"Hey, Tim," Mike said just as I was about to head off to Science Club. "We should really hang out more."

I knew it would never happen, but I was flattered nonetheless. "Yeah, that'd be great, Mikey."

He fake-punched me in the upper arm, an affectionate gesture that nearly knocked me over. He laughed and said, "You know, Tim, you're the only one who ever called me that. I kinda miss that."

Apparently there was a chance I would actually spend some time with Mike, as his interest seemed genuine. I was already calculating the benefits of being seen with a football jock, not the least of which would be hanging onto my lunch money till lunch time.

"Maybe we can even room together on the science field trip," he offered.

"Science field trip?" I asked. "What science field trip?"

"The one Ma Barker's got going."

"Oh? That's funny. She hasn't mentioned it in our biology class."

"Maybe it's not for the brainiacs," he said. "But it sounds kinda cool. We're going to Kentucky. Or was it Kansas? Some kind of museum anyway."

"Sounds good," I said. "Look, Mikey, I've got to get going. Science Club."

"Oh, yeah, and I got football practice. Coach Braun gets real mean if we're late."

"I can imagine," I said.

"OK, see you around, Tim."

"Yeah, Mike, you take care."

And he was off. I watched him disappear down the hall with no small amazement: how could someone so big move so fast? And without knocking anyone down like bowling pins? He was actually … elegant in his motions.

But what was foremost on my mind was Mrs. Barker's field trip. What was in Kentucky—or Kansas for that matter—that warranted an overnight field trip? Did they even *have* museums in either state? No, I decided, Mike probably just got it wrong. He might be a fine athlete, but he isn't the brightest bulb in the marquee. By the time I got to Science Club I'd set aside all thought of Mrs. Barker, field trips and states that start with a K and concentrated on the discussion of our semester project: were we going to build an emission-free race car, a solar-powered hovercraft or a fighting robot? Predictably, the robot won.

Back home I nuked some left-over lasagna from the previous day's family meal and went up to my room to do my homework, an essay on Hemingway for Ms. Pewney. It took longer than I expected, as I got overly involved in some research on the Spanish Civil War, ingesting far more information than I could ever possibly use in my essay, and probably my lifetime. That's usually how homework goes with me. The actual time spent on assignments is, to put it generously, minimal, whereas extraneous private research generally proves quite time-consuming. I wondered whether Mike Petersson put in anything like the hours I did, and had to think it terribly unfair that, no matter how hard he worked, he would no doubt end up heaving refrigerators around a warehouse somewhere.

As I was about to turn in for the night, not having spoken to or even seen a living soul since arriving home, I suddenly remembered the field trip Mike had mentioned. Thinking a state like Kentucky (or Kansas) probably didn't have more than half a dozen museums to call its own, I plugged two simple words into Google: "museum" and "Kentucky." Within milliseconds I had to admit that I had clearly done Kentucky a disservice; my search yielded over nine million results! Even allowing for multiple entries for the same place and sentences like "We left Kentucky to go to a museum," the state obviously had far more such institutions than I had been willing to give it credit for.

The Louisville Science Center sounded like a worthy destination for a school field trip, as did the apparently much smaller East Kentucky Science Center. As fascinating as I'm sure the Kentucky Derby Museum, the Oscar Getz Museum of Whiskey History and the National Corvette Museum are, I couldn't quite imagine that Mrs. Barker was taking her science students to any of them. I decided to narrow my search to include the word "science." To my dismay, the very first result beamed to me from Mountain View, California, was something called the Creation Museum, located in Petersburg, Kentucky.

Surely that was not Mrs. Barker's destination! And maybe it wasn't as bad as I thought. But the museum's home page read like a parody of itself. "Welcome and prepare to believe," it proclaimed. And it got worse: "The state-of-the-art 70,000 square foot museum brings the pages of the Bible to life, casting its characters and animals in dynamic form and placing them in familiar settings. Adam and Eve live in the Garden of Eden. Children play and dinosaurs roam near Eden's Rivers. The serpent coils cunningly in the Tree of the Knowledge of Good and Evil. Majestic murals, great masterpieces brimming with pulsating colors and details, provide a backdrop for many of the settings."

This was as much of a museum as the Magic Kingdom at Disney World was! "Children play and dinosaurs roam"?! The dinosaurs died out more than 60 million years before the first creature that could be classified as even remotely human walked the earth. This "museum" was not an educational effort; its purpose was to spread misinformation and perpetuate ignorance. If this was where Mrs. Barker was taking her class, she had to be stopped.

Chapter 11

Storm Clouds Gather

I was just getting used to the pause in the perpetual pounding from primitive punks when it was suddenly and surprisingly terminated the following Monday morning by a stray leg that tripped me on my way up the stairs to homeroom. I didn't see who the leg belonged to, but there were any number of candidates in the vicinity and plenty of kids laughing at my misfortune as I picked up what was left of my dignity and belongings from the faux granite steps.

As luck would have it, one of the people to come along while I was gathering up my things was Mike Petersson. The crowd of amused onlookers dispersed pretty quickly when Mike started to help me locate the last of my writing implements.

"You gotta be more careful, Tim," my savior said. "These steps can be pretty slippery." It never would have occurred to Mike in his blissful innocence that I hadn't tripped of my own accord.

"Yeah, I will, Mikey. And thanks for helping me with my stuff."

"No prob. Hey, I gotta go. My homeroom's way on the other end of the building. See ya."

Once again I was amazed by Mike's speed as he dodged his way through the crowd, trying to make it to homeroom before the bell. I supposed that was why he was so successful at football. Then I remembered that I, too, had to be in my own homeroom before the bell, even though I thought Miss Gaunt would probably go easy on me. I sensed that I was rapidly becoming one of her favorites, though I should like to point out that I had done nothing out of the ordinary to garner her favor.

The bell rang to signal the start of homeroom just as I reached the door to Room 421. I put on my most charming smile as I turned the knob and entered. But it wasn't Miss Gaunt who awaited me behind the door and in front of the class, but a very large African American man of indeterminate age and unfriendly disposition.

"Name?" the man snarled, looking at me aggressively.

"Timothy Thompson." I wanted to ask who he was, but I refrained.

"You're late, Timothy Thompson, and I don't like it when students are late."

I did my best to show regret and disguise my annoyance. I was, after all, no more than five seconds late, and the delay hadn't even been my fault. Nonetheless, I kept my own counsel as the teacher mellowed slightly and introduced himself.

"As I was about to tell you when I was interrupted by the late arrival," he said, casting a scowl in my direction, "my name is Mr. Wilson. I teach mechanical drafting and Latin, and I'm taking over for Miss Gaunt, who has now officially retired. I met with Miss Gaunt last period on Friday, right after Principal Powers hired me.

"She was, as she put it, 'relieved to be relieved,' and she asked me to extend her apologies for not being able to say good-bye to all of you. She did say she would come to visit when she returns from her round-the-world cruise, which she booked even as we were meeting." With a glance at his watch, which I noticed was incongruously small for a man his size, he chuckled and added that Miss Gaunt would be boarding a ship for the first leg of her journey in Fort Lauderdale that very morning. "Quite a gal, that Miss Gaunt."

Mr. Wilson's apparent fondness for Miss Gaunt raised my estimation of the man somewhat, though I would have been loath to call her "quite a gal." The man's feelings were obviously genuine, for he proceeded to relate much of the contents of his chat with Miss Gaunt, which mostly involved her plans to hike the Inca Trail in Peru and to bathe in the Ganges River in India. She had also wanted to run with the bulls in Pamplona, but that happens in the summer, so she'd have to do that some other time. As preposterous as these things sounded for someone who must be pushing 70—but from which side?—they somehow fit my image of my former homeroom teacher. Yes, she's quite a gal, and I was going to miss her.

Mr. Wilson's narrative ended in time for him to take the roll. When he came to my name, he said in an ominous tone, "And I know Timothy Thompson is here," and he made some sort of mark next to my name. This could not be good, I knew, but the bell rang before I could dwell on it, and I had to rush off to Mr. Leitner's social studies class. I didn't want to be late for another class, so I avoided letter sweaters, cheerleader uniforms and other signs of possible hostiles and watched my every step to make certain I would not be tripped up again. The day had already got off to a bad start: the tripping incident and losing my beloved homeroom teacher—so I was determined to make sure things improved from there on in. Ever the optimist!

I made it to Mr. Leitner's classroom with time to spare, so unlike many of my classmates I had everything I needed on my desk and sat at the ready before the bell. Once everyone was settled, which, I thought, couldn't have taken longer in a room full of six-year-olds who had all forgotten to take their Ritalin™, Mr. Leitner began.

"You will recall that, at the end of class on Friday, we conducted a straw poll on the topic of obedience and resistance."

A number of students shifted uncomfortably in their seats because they, in fact, had no such recollection. Mr. Leitner seemed to sense that, for he proceeded to present the premise and the results.

"The class was more or less equally divided on the question of whether it was a right, a duty, or, on the contrary, plainly illegal to disobey laws that we, as citizens, perceived as unjust."

Joel Tupero's hand shot up. Joel was our resident anarchist; at least that's how he described himself. Apparently the irony of an anarchist who raised his hand in class to register an objection was lost on Joel, but then again, most things were.

"Yes, Mr. Tupero, I was just getting to your ... erm ... minority opinion. There was also one vote in favor of permanent resistance to all laws."

Joel lowered his hand and looked quite satisfied with himself, then put his head demonstratively down on his desk, having done his bit for the cause that day.

"Now," Mr. Leitner continued, "let's get concrete. In this state, there's a law that requires everyone traveling in a car to wear a seatbelt. How many of you would say that citizens have the duty or the right to disobey that particular law?"

Two hands went up. One of them was Joel Tupero's, so it didn't really count. The other belonged to a girl so plain that even I couldn't remember her name. Apparently Mr. Leitner couldn't either because he deviated from his habit of calling everyone Mr. or Ms. So-and-So and simply nodded in her direction.

The girl looked flustered and said, "I didn't know I was going to have to say anything. I'd like to change my vote." When it became clear to Ms. No-Name that Mr. Leitner still expected her to explain her stance, she stated, "It's a stupid law, the seatbelt thing. I mean, like, seatbelts can totally ruin your clothes."

"I see," remarked Mr. Leitner. "So you're saying that the fact that a seatbelt can like totally ruin your clothes, by which you no doubt mean wrinkle, gives you the right not to wear one? To break the law?"

"Well, yes," Ms. NN answered, though she sounded less sure of herself. Mr. Leitner let it go and offered up his next law for our resistance.

"Next example: the state legislature is once again considering a bill that would require everyone riding a motorcycle to wear an approved helmet. If the bill passes, who thinks they have the right—or the duty—to not wear a helmet?"

Significantly more hands went up this time, most of them male, including, of course, Joel Tupero's, but not, interestingly, Ms. NN's. Mr. Leitner called on one of the boys, Jesús Espinoza, and asked him to explain his stance. Jesús was generally quite eloquent, so I was curious as to his answer.

"To me, it's all about individual freedoms," Jesús began. "We have to watch out how much of our individual liberty we're willing to hand over to the government."

Made sense to me, but Mr. Leitner wasn't satisfied. "Yet you didn't have any particular feelings about giving up your individual freedom to not wear a seatbelt. Why is that, Mr. Espinoza?"

After a slight hesitation, Jesús conceded, "Because I was only thinking of myself, my own needs. It doesn't bother me to put on a seatbelt, but when I get on the back of my brother's motorcycle, I like the feel of the wind in my hair. I don't see why the state should be able to take that away from me. So I'd like to change my vote on the seatbelt question, give more respect to other people's personal freedoms."

The general assent, including, I am embarrassed to admit, my own, amounted to a roar, but Mr. Leitner spoke over it. "So you're saying, Mr. Espinoza—and all who agree with him—that the feel of wind in your hair outweighs your responsibility to the state?"

Jesús looked puzzled. "You mean my responsibility to obey a silly law? Yes, I do think that."

But Mr. Leitner was going for blood. "So the state has no right to protect its citizens?"

"From themselves? No."

"And if a cyclist has horrible head injuries because he wasn't wearing a helmet?"

"I would say that was his choice," Jesús pronounced firmly.

Mr. Leitner went for the jugular. "So the state would be within its rights to let that cyclist die? After all, it was his choice to crack open his skull, his personal freedom to spread his gray matter all over the highway."

"No," Jesús protested over the general hubbub that ensued after Mr. Leitner's outrageous suggestion. "Of course not. It's still the responsibility of the state to take care of its citizens."

"Ay, there's the rub, as the Bard would have said. So you're saying that the state has the obligation to take care of this unfortunate traffic casualty, even though he is, in fact, a victim of his own stupidity."

At this point Jesús seemed to have an inkling where this was going, but he bravely affirmed that this was indeed the state's responsibility.

"So the entire cost of scraping this guy's brains off the pavement, transporting him to hospital, emergency room, ICU, and if he lives, dozens of operations and probably months or even years of physical therapy, speech therapy, occupational therapy and what not—all that is the state's responsibility?"

"Or his insurance company's, yes."

"So either way, it costs me money," Mr. Leitner said glumly.

"I'm not following you, Mr. Leitner. Why does it cost *you* money?"

"I pay insurance premiums. I pay taxes. Ultimately it's people like me who are paying for *your* individual freedom to feel the wind in your hair."

The room grew silent as the wind was taken out of our sails and some of the consequences of "freedom" sank in. Mr. Leitner proceeded to write the words "Rights" and "Responsibilities" on the board. He turned to look at the class. Some of us were nodding pensively, others looking annoyed. Mr. Leitner took this in with a slight grin, then turned back to the board and wrote two more words: "Obedience" and "Resistance." He then connected all four words with arrows pointing in both directions.

"One of our tasks this semester," he said while completing his work of art, then turning to face us again, "will be to look at events in our nation's history, as well as some current affairs, to examine the dynamic I have just drawn on the board. How do we as citizens balance rights and responsibilities?

"What factors influence our responsibility to obey or our right to resist? And are there circumstances that could conceivably make resistance a citizen's responsibility?

"For tomorrow I'd like you to take a first stab at formulating some statements about this dynamic. I suggest you start with something a little closer to home than our seatbelt or helmet examples. Something that affects you. Maybe something to do with school. I don't know, a school rule that seems overly restrictive, for example. Or a teacher who inserts his or her own point of view into their lessons, like an English teacher who teaches an obscure and not generally accepted theory about the origins of Shakespeare's plays."

Something about that last example suggested that Mr. Leitner might be referring to Ma Barker: "origins"? "not generally accepted theory"? If that didn't describe her attempt to introduce creationist theory into her biology class, what did? But then came the zinger.

"Or another example: a U.S. history teacher who refuses to deal with the Second World War because he doesn't like what it says about America's role in the world."

Or a biology teacher who refused to teach her students about evolution, I thought.

"Would that be acceptable?" Mr. Leitner continued. "Would such an important omission give students the right—or even the responsibility—to resist? Think about those questions and try to come up with five statements about rights and responsibilities, obedience and resistance by tomorrow so we can discuss them in class."

Mr. Leitner's timing was, as usual, perfect: the bell rang right after he finished formulating his homework assignment. It had been a stimulating discussion, but I left the classroom with the very uneasy feeling that Mr. Leitner had been trying to tell me something. He hadn't cast me any significant looks. In fact, if anything I'd say he had been trying to avoid eye contact with me, which I knew could also convey meaning.

But what?

Chapter 12

Worst. Day. Ever. (So Far)

After the discussion of rights, responsibilities and revolution in social studies, I went to phy ed with more than my usual apprehension. Nothing terribly out of the ordinary happened in Gym that day, however, other than the fact that I was a bit distracted and wasn't really following Coach Braun's instructions for a basketball relay and, when it was my turn, ran left instead of right. Coach Braun derided me in front of everyone—"Thompson, for somebody who's supposed to be smart, you sure do act stupid"—but that was a mild reprimand coming from him, hardly worth the notice.

Still, I was terribly preoccupied when I went to biology, not a particularly good state to be in when the use of sharp instruments is to be expected. Mrs. Barker had announced the previous week that we would be dissecting earthworms this lesson, which made a number of people doubly squeamish: not only would they be cutting open an animal carcass for the first time, they would have to touch the same slimy, reprehensible creatures that naughty boys had been taunting little girls with since time immemorial.

Megan Cho, who was still averse to the idea of dissection, actually asked me to be her lab partner, which was absolutely fine with me. I had hoped to get closer to her this school year, and if it wasn't meant to be brought about by anything more romantic than *Lumbricus terrestris* (the scientific name for the earthworm), so be it. I believe in coming to class prepared, so I had read extensively about the earthworm and done a virtual dissection online over the weekend. I had even rehearsed how I might comfort Megan through the trauma of slicing open a once-living being. Needless to say, at the end of each scenario I went through, Megan was my girlfriend for life. Would that life were as easy as fantasy!

At the beginning of the period, Mrs. Barker assigned us to our lab tables and briefly instructed us on the use of safety goggles, aprons and gloves as well as the proper way to hold the scalpel, forceps and dissecting probe. She also gave us our worksheets, which contained a rudimentary sketch of an opened worm that we were to expand on and a list of features and organs which we were to identify and label. Two of the bits were the anus and clitellum, sources of much amusement for some of the less mature boys.

[Aside: The clitellum is the thick ring toward the anterior (front) of the worm. Although it does in fact play a role in earthworm reproduction, the fact that the first four letters of its name are shared by a part of the human female anatomy is mere coincidence. Let the record show that I am frequently disgusted by many of the individuals I share my gender with.]

Through division of labor, Megan and I were making excellent progress: I was doing the cutting, Megan the diagramming and labeling. As small as the worm was, it was difficult to isolate the digestive and the circulatory systems, which got me wondering whether things wouldn't get easier once we progressed to dissecting a frog or, better yet, a pig. Bigger animals. Higher animals. More evolved animals. With revolution and evolution on the brain, I suddenly had an idea.

"Mrs. Barker?" I called in my most innocent and charming voice as she passed our lab table.

"Yes, Timothy, what is it?" she asked unsuspectingly.

"Well, looking at the earthworm's primitive digestive system," I began, "I was wondering where exactly on the evolutionary scale it belongs."

Mrs. Barker looked ever-so-slightly irritated by my line of inquiry. "I'm not quite sure I understand what you're asking."

"Two things, really. First of all, I was wondering when the earthworm might have evolved."

Actually, I had found the answer to that question on the Internet over the previous weekend: it's complicated. Because worms and their relatives have soft bodies, they don't leave a whole lot behind when they expire, but the fossil record suggests that earthworms were burrowing around at least as early as 250 million years ago, give or take a few million. If Mrs. Barker believed the earth was less than 10,000 years old, as many creationists do, she could hardly give me a scientifically accepted response.

"I wouldn't know," she replied drily.

My next question was a genuine one, for I had spent hours reading scientific texts that I'd downloaded without finding a clear solution. "Maybe you can help me with my next problem," I offered.

Mrs. Barker glared at me.

"We've discovered that the earthworm has a gizzard. Do you happen to know whether it evolved separately from other animals with gizzards? You know, birds and fish and reptiles?"

"No, I can't help you there either, I'm afraid."

As the teacher started to turn away, I pushed a bit harder—too hard, as it turned out. "All this would be so much easier to put in context if we'd only done evolution beforehand."

Whereas no one had been paying more than peripheral attention at best to my conversation with Mrs. Barker, I detected a change in the room. Dissection tools were no longer cutting and probing, pens no longer jotting down notes, quiet conversations ceased. Everyone was poised to hear how our biology teacher reacted to this implicit criticism of her curriculum planning. Megan looked horrified, but I thought I saw a twinge of admiration in her expression of horror.

"Are you questioning my teaching methods, Timothy?"

"No, Mrs. Barker," I assured her. "It's just that, on the first day of class, you said we'd be studying the origins of the species before we started looking at individual animals." I deliberately "adapted" her words. In fact she had not taken the words "origins of the species," which would have been too reminiscent of Darwin for her liking, into her mouth, but had instead spoken of "different theories of how so many different life forms came into being." My rewording had its desired effect.

"I'm sure I didn't say anything of the kind," Mrs. Barker proclaimed, somewhat huffily. "I had been planning a discussion of different theories of how life and species came to be. But *you* prevented that from happening."

"Does that mean we won't be talking about evolution at all?"

"Yes, Timothy, that's exactly what it means," she snapped at me. "If I can't present what I believe to be true, I'm certainly not going to teach you something I disagree with."

There it was. A biology teacher who wasn't going to teach the theory that most scientists consider central to an understanding of the subject. Although I had suspected as much, I was flabbergasted by this admission. That's when I slipped up.

"You can't be serious."

I realized my mistake when I heard Megan gasp. Yes, I had wanted to challenge Mrs. Barker, but I hadn't meant to be disrespectful.

Mrs. Barker shifted her stance. She stood straight, her legs apart, her body toward me, arms crossed in front of her chest—an aggressive stance if ever there was one. "I beg your pardon?" she intoned in a most deliberate manner. I noted her nostrils widening and was reminded of a cartoon bull about to charge. The tiny grin that formed on my face at that wasn't lost on Mrs. Barker.

"You think this is funny?"

"No, I … What I meant was …" What could I say to explain myself without digging myself in deeper? "I mean …" I blathered like this for what seemed like several minutes but probably amounted to little more than a few seconds. Mrs. Barker was obviously livid.

"I say we continue this with Mr. Powers. Go to his office and wait for me there."

And so I, Timothy Thompson, model student, was sent to the principal's office for the first time in my life.

Chapter 13

Meeting Mr. Powers

I must have been very pale when I arrived at the school's main office, for the secretary, before I could say why I was there, clucked over me and started filling out a form for going home sick. Apparently students could show the form to the police if they were stopped on suspicion of truancy. I briefly wondered how much a pad of those forms was worth on the black market, but was then taken aback that I should be having such thoughts at all. Apparently my brush with the law in the form of an angry teacher was enough to start me off on a life of crime, and I vowed to discuss my dark side, hitherto unknown to me, with Dr. Feelgood at our next appointment.

The secretary quickly changed her tune—from clucking to tisking—once I told her the real reason for my visit to her lair. She pulled my file and commanded me to wait in the most uncomfortable chair I had ever sat in. I tried hard not to fidget because every time I shifted my position, the secretary looked up from her computer keyboard and tisked again. I found it most disquieting.

After a few minutes, Mr. Powers came out and called to me: "Timothy Thompson? Come in here, please."

I leapt up and headed towards the principal's office, grateful for the opportunity to tell Mr. Powers what had happened before Mrs. Barker arrived. I hadn't seen the man since the "Welcome Rally" on my first day, and from up close I could detect warmth and kindness in his demeanor, although he was making every effort to look stern. Principal Powers closed the door behind us and motioned for me to sit, this time in a very comfortable armchair. He sat down behind his antique desk, which was probably even older than him, and folded his hands in front of him.

"I've been looking at your file, Timothy," he said gently. "It seems you've never been in trouble before." Although it was technically a statement, his voice rose at the end to indicate that he expected a response.

"No, sir."

"Why now? Does this have anything to do with that movie business two weeks ago?"

"No, not directly, Mr. Powers."

"Indirectly then?"

"Yes, Mr. Powers. Indirectly."

Mr. Powers drew a deep breath, but he smiled at me and said, "Timothy, I like a guessing game as much as the next person, but it would be most helpful if you could just tell me what happened. Mrs. Barker will be here soon; then she can give me her version of why she sent you here."

"Yes, sorry, sir," I began. I then proceeded to give him an objective description and verbatim account of my exchange with Mrs. Barker, adding only my motivations and lack of desire to offend. I didn't want to mention the cartoon bull, so I stretched the truth slightly and said I'd grinned due to nervousness.

"That was a stellar account, Timothy," Mr. Powers said. "Very detailed. I assume it's accurate?"

"Oh, yes, sir."

"Hmm, it says in your file that you have an eidetic memory. Is that true?"

"No, not really. I've never been diagnosed, but from what I've read, what I have is more like hyperthymesia."

"Hyperthymesia? An interesting word. *Hyper*, being Greek for 'over, above and beyond,' and *thymesia*, from Greek *thymesis*, meaning 'memory.' But presumably you know that."

"Yes, sir. You know Greek?"

"I used to teach ancient Greek and history," Mr. Powers said, almost whimsically. Then he chortled and said, "And if the rumors are correct, I was a contemporary of Socrates! Or don't the kids tell that one any more?"

"I haven't heard it, Mr. Powers."

"Hmph. Must be because I no longer teach Greek. I suppose now they just say that I came over on the *Mayflower*."

"Yes, I've heard that," I said and fidgeted uncomfortably.

"You really don't lie, do you? Most students wouldn't admit that they'd been privy to rumors like that.—But tell me, how exactly does hyperthymesia manifest itself?"

"Well, it refers to autobiographical memory. Basically, people with hyperthymesia can remember everything they've ever experienced from a certain age onward."

"So, everything you've ever done, seen, heard or read, is committed to your memory? Fascinating! But how is that different from eidetic memory?"

"Well, people with an eidetic memory have total recall, too, but eventually their memories fade. Mine stay with me, whether I want them to or not."

Mr. Powers and I had just finished our little discourse on my mnemonic abilities when Mrs. Barker arrived.

"Mrs. Barker," Mr. Powers greeted my still-enraged biology teacher, "Timothy here was just telling me what happened in your biology class this morning. Timothy, is there anything you'd like to say to Mrs. Barker?"

"Yes, sir.—I'm really sorry, Mrs. Barker. I didn't mean to be disrespectful."

Mrs. Barker didn't react to my apology, but instead looked at Mr. Powers, puzzled and angry at the same time. "Don't you want to hear what happened?" Her nostrils were flaring again.

"Timothy has already told me, but by all means, please tell me your version, Mrs. Barker."

She proceeded to do precisely that, embellishing here and there to make me sound more evil. Or she simply reported it as she remembered it, not being endowed with a perfect memory. Mr. Powers listened attentively, nodding several times as Mrs. Barker spoke. He furrowed his brow in concentration as she went to great lengths to describe the "sneering grin" I'd supposedly cast her after my provocations.

"Thank you, Mrs. Barker. Timothy's account coincides with yours in all the salient details," Mr. Powers said. Then looking benevolently in my direction, he added, "As I'd expected. Timothy, why don't you tell Mrs. Barker what you told me about the grin?"

"Right. You see, Mrs. Barker, I always get this stupid grin on my face when I'm nervous." To underscore my little fabrication, I heaped on another: "I often get in trouble with my mother for the same reason, but I really didn't mean anything by it."

"I see." Mrs. Barker mellowed somewhat. "But you did say 'You can't be serious.' How do you explain that?"

"I can't explain it, Mrs. Barker. I was surprised when you said you weren't going to teach us about evolution, and it slipped out. I shouldn't have said it, and I'm sorry."

Mrs. Barker pursed her lips and grew silent for a moment. Again, I had a cartoon image in my head, this time of gears spinning in her head as she thought. I successfully suppressed another grin.

"OK," Mrs. Barker said. "Apology accepted."

"Excellent," Mr. Powers pronounced. "And we won't be seeing any repeats, will we, Timothy?"

"No, sir!" I said hastily, although I wondered whether I'd be able to feign respect for this woman. I'd been brought up to respect my elders, but my parents had also instilled in me a strong sense that I should challenge authority when convinced those in authority were in the wrong. Where, after all, would our country be if Rosa Parks hadn't stood up to that Montgomery bus driver, if the unions hadn't taken to the streets against the robber barons, if the Founders hadn't been willing to wage war against King George III?

"Very well then," Mr. Powers said. "If there's nothing else, I wish you both a stellar day."

There *was* something else, the proverbial elephant in the room: my biology teacher was unwilling to teach the subject properly. She was allowing her religious beliefs to trump scientific reason, and I found that completely unacceptable. The situation needed to be addressed.

"There is one other thing, Mr. Powers," I said, already regretting it. Mrs. Barker glared at me.

"What's that, Timothy?"

My mind was racing. I truly didn't want to destroy the conciliatory atmosphere. "I'm late for my German class," I said, feeling like a coward. "Could I have some sort of pass, please?"

I thought I detected relief from both the adults in the room.

"Of course, Timothy. Just ask Mrs. McDermitt on your way out."

So *that* was the secretary's name; she was the infamous Mrs. McDoormat, so called because you had to get past her to gain access to Principal Powers. Students who spent a lot of time in the principal's office often talked about her. She had quite a reputation at school. Rumored to have once been a TSA security guard or, alternatively, an interrogator at the Guantánamo Bay detention camp, she was said to possess Darth Vader-like powers. I worried that, if I followed the path set by my own dark side, I would be seeing more of her. On some level, of course, I was aware that she was not actually capable of choking people by force of will with some sort of Jedi death grip, but I didn't care to test it.

Mrs. McDermitt handed me the late slip without comment—indeed, without looking up from her work—as I passed.

Chapter 14

Rebel With A Cause

After my brush with the law, my friends were eager to hear my report. None of them, of course, had ever been sent to the principal's office, so I was somewhat of a celebrity amongst the nerdy crowd—still one of them, but set apart through my notoriety. I had, after all, been up close and personal with the ultimate head of discipline at Omar L. Batshit High School.

"Is Principal Powers as old as they say?"

"Is it true they have cells in the main office?"

"Did Mrs. McDoormat fix you with her evil eye?"

It was Megan—my Megan—who shushed them all and asked the insightful question that I could deal with. "What happened when you went to Mr. Powers' office, Timothy?"

I gave them a quick account of events between bites of mystery meat (billed as "succulent tenders of beef")—I'd been feeling adventurous as I went through the cafeteria line. For some reason, I was ravenously hungry. Apparently walking on the wild side was a good way to work up an appetite.

When I finished telling my story, Megan, who along with Josh had already supplied the details of my classroom encounter with Mrs. Barker, said and did something I hadn't expected but had often lain awake nights hoping for. She put her hand on top of mine and said, "I'm so proud of you, Timothy Thompson." The others interpreted her gesture differently than I did: they put their hands on top of hers and turned it into a Musketeer pact group-handshake.

In the end, Josh was the last one to withdraw his hand. He left it on top of mine just long enough for me to find it a little awkward, then squeezed and said, "Yeah, Timothy, we're all proud."

"Thanks, guys," I said. "But what do we do now?"

Clem seemed confused. "What do you mean? You already stopped Ma Barker from teaching intelligent design, and now you're a hero for challenging her during class. I'd say that's pretty good already."

Again it was Megan who understood me better than everyone else. "I think what's bothering Timothy is that Mrs. Barker still isn't planning to teach our class about evolution."

"But you already know about evolution," Stuart said. "So what's the difference?"

I looked around the table, dumbfounded by Stuart's question. He sat there staring at me, his lower jaw almost meeting his chest, half-chewed "Salvatore's spicy sausage pizza" on display in his open mouth. Josh and Clem looked no less mystified, Lamont merely curious. Megan's expression was one of support. I sensed that she would have liked to answer Stuart's provocation herself, but was holding back for me to do so.

"'What's the difference?' you ask. There are twenty-six students in that biology class, and I think they all have the right to a proper education. And since it's an AP course and we're all hoping to get college credit for it, I'd say it's pretty damned important that the teacher teaches a central tenet of the subject."

My use of an expletive clearly rattled Josh. I'm sure he didn't hear words like *damn* in his Bible-thumping home. (I am aware that *Bible-thumping* is a derogatory term, but I rather like the image. Apologies to all who take offense!) "OK," he said, "I take your point. But it's not like we can force her to teach something she doesn't believe."

"Maybe we can," Lamont said. "Or the courts can. I mean, she works for the state, not for some church."

Clem looked skeptical. "There *is* this little thing called the First Amendment—you know, freedom of speech and all that. I don't think anybody can force her to say anything."

"But what about *our* right to an education?" I asked. "It seems there are two different rights competing with each other."

"That's what the courts are for," Megan stated perceptively. "You're going to have to ask your mother, Timothy."

And that's what I did.

"She said *what*?!" My mother was outraged when I told her about Mrs. Barker's refusal to teach evolution. "I can't believe she said that!"

"My friends and I were thinking that maybe we could force her."

Mother immediately went into lawyer mode. "That could prove difficult," she said pensively, "from a purely legal standpoint. Any lawsuit would have to be against the school district, not her. Although she could, of course, be named. Then we'd have to name Mr. Powers as well. But I don't think he'd take it personally. It's probably best to threaten a suit rather than file it right away …"

I found the chain of thought fascinating and thought for the first time that a career in law might just be for me. But I didn't particularly like the idea of naming Mr. Powers in a lawsuit. He's such a nice man, and I thought he and I had established some rapport. I kept my doubts to myself for the time being.

"I'll need to do some research, Timothy," Mom said, "and we'll revisit the topic in a day or two if that's all right with you."

"Sure, Mom. Thanks," I said. "Can I help with the research?"

"Yes, that would be a great help. Why don't you check into the state curriculum for biology and let me know what it says with regard to evolution?"

I set about it immediately.

It wasn't difficult to find what Mother needed, but it wasn't as easy as one might think. Probably to avoid controversy, the State Board of Education—the cowards—made no mention of "evolution" in their so-called "Learning Standards." "Darwin" did not feature either. I supposed this was meant to stymie the efforts of particularly lazy creationists who couldn't be bothered to do any more than plug "evolution" or "Darwin" into a search engine in their quest for quarry. Anyone more determined could find what they needed easily enough.

The Standards *were* clear, however: they explicitly stated that "students who meet the standard know and apply concepts that explain how living things function, adapt and change." The "fossil record" was mentioned as well. They didn't need to mention Darwin or evolution; "a rose by any other name would smell as sweet," as the Bard wrote (Shakespeare, *Romeo and Juliet*, Act II, Scene 2).

Anticipating my mother's next question, I checked to see what status the "Learning Standards" had. Were they requirements or recommendations? The first indication I found read as follows: "The Illinois Learning Standards define what all students in all Illinois public schools should know and be able to do." The modal "should" sounded pretty vague to me, so I kept looking. And looking. And looking. Everything I found was written in an obscure language known as legalese; the idea of a law career was looking less attractive by the hour.

Mother seemed very satisfied with the meager results of my research. "Excellent, Timothy. With this we can make a very good case for forcing your teacher either to teach evolution or to resign.

"But just so you know: this could get very unpleasant. And there are no guarantees."

"But you said we had what we needed to make a case," I protested.

"Well, that's the thing about the law: making a case isn't the same as winning—no matter how good your case is. There are some pretty complicated issues involved here. And I suspect your teacher has an ace or two up her sleeve."

"How so?"

"It's possible that she's expecting a lawsuit and already has financial backers lined up."

"Financial backers?"

"Yes, in case this thing goes to court. With appeals it can take a long time and get very expensive. Some of these Christian groups are well-organized—good lawyers, unlimited resources. As far as I could tell in the short time I've been looking at it, there hasn't been a case of this kind before."

"I thought the courts had already decided you can't teach creationism or ID in schools."

"They have, and you can't. But it doesn't look like anybody has ever tried to force the teaching of evolution. That's a whole new kettle of fish, and it's hard to say how it might go. It could be the other side wants to force the issue and settle it once and for all.

"But let's not get ahead of ourselves. I'll talk to your principal tomorrow."

"Yeah, about that …" I hadn't told my parents about being sent to the principal's office or my chat with Principal Powers. I quickly filled Mother in and waited for her to explode at her delinquent son.

Instead of exploding, she simply said, "Then they won't be taken by surprise. Both your teacher and Mr. Powers know it's an issue."

"So you aren't mad at me?"

"For standing up for your beliefs? Of course not. In fact, I'm proud of you, Timothy."

I had no memory of my mother ever saying she was proud of me, so it had probably never happened before. It was a good feeling, and as I was trying to go to sleep that night, I reflected on it at length.

Apparently all I had needed to earn my mother's pride and admiration was to rebel. Had I known, perhaps I could have tried rebelling sooner. But rebelling for its own sake wasn't for me; I wasn't cut out to be a "rebel without a cause," despite the poster of James Dean (an actor and the ultimate cool dude, died in 1955) on my bedroom wall.

Chapter 15

New Friends

Mother asked for and was granted an appointment with Principal Powers the next day. She informed Mr. Powers in advance what it was concerning and suggested that Mrs. Barker join them. I felt more than a little apprehensive about my third-period biology class, but I couldn't detect any negative vibes from Mrs. Barker. However, at the end of class she asked me to stay "for a minute."

"As you know," she began, "I'll be meeting with your mother and Mr. Powers this afternoon at 3 o'clock."

I didn't actually know the exact time, but I nodded agreement.

"I know you think I should be teaching you about Darwinian theory, Timothy. But I can't do that. It would be totally against my convictions to teach only a theory that violates what I believe in. If I could present both sides of the controversy within the scientific community, it would be a different story, but that, apparently, isn't allowed."

"I understand, Mrs. Barker," I replied.

"Good," she said cheerily. "I wouldn't want this whole thing to be a problem between us."

I was starting to think Mother was right: Mrs. Barker *did* have an agenda; she wanted this to come to a lawsuit. "I'm glad you're not taking it personally," I told her. "I like you, and I think you're a good teacher."

"Thank you, Timothy. But you think I'm wrong about Darwin."

"Well, yes. There doesn't really seem to be much of a controversy. I can't find many scientists who agree with you."

"Just because intelligent design is a minority opinion doesn't make it wrong," she countered. "There was a time when a majority of scientists thought the sun revolved around the earth."

I was relieved to hear that she didn't think *that*, or that the earth was flat and the moon made of green cheese. To me all those myths were on the same level as the creation story.

"Anyway," Mrs. Barker continued, "I just wanted to make sure that we can still be friends."

I didn't quite know how to judge her last remark, as I'd never considered her a friend in the first place. Come to think of it, I'd never even thought of the teachers I liked and respected as my friends. Yes, I liked Mr. Grass, and I found him friendly, but a friend? I muttered something along the lines of "No worries" and left as quickly as I could without being rude. I was going to be late for German—again—but I didn't want to ask my new friend for a late slip, preferring instead to risk the wrath of Mr. Pfister and finding myself in detention.

Although I arrived almost two minutes late for fourth period, Mr. Pfister—no, I did not make up the rhyming name—merely nodded at me as I took my seat. (German was my weakest subject, but he had told me I was his best student ever, so I suppose he was willing to give me a little leeway.) Class was as normal as could be expected of a language that was obviously designed to subjugate an entire nation and make it susceptible to the siren song of a strong leader. I suspected that, even today, the German *Volk* would blindly follow anyone who promised to free them from the yoke of three genders and four grammatical cases. Could anyone, I wondered, possibly achieve a degree of fluency in this dreadful tongue, or did the Germans stutter their way through life while trying to work out whether the next word they needed to utter was *der, die* or *das*—or indeed *den* or *dem*. And Mr. Pfister had already hinted that he was protecting us from further indignities. I was looking forward to lunch.

When I met my friends they were, of course, curious to hear what my mother had said about making Mrs. Barker teach evolution. I duly reported between bites of the pulled pork sandwich Dad had packed for me. As we were talking, I thought I saw several people staring at us. While one of them was wearing a letter sweater and, as such, appeared dangerous, most of the gawkers looked innocuous enough, so I finally decided I was imagining things. That changed when two of them, a "green"-looking boy and girl who had been sitting together, shyly—almost apprehensively—approached our table.

The pair stood at one end of the table. The boy cleared his throat audibly. "We just want to let you know that we're praying for you," the boy said.

After an awkward pause, the girl spoke. "Jesus is your friend. He loves you—no matter what."

Without further ado, the odd couple disappeared into the lunchroom hubbub.

My friends and I sat staring toward the spot where the boy and girl had been standing, stunned to silence. Stuart was the first to speak.

"Double-U T F?"

Clem was next. "Did that just happen?"

Followed by Josh: "PTL."

"PTL?" I asked.

"It seemed appropriate," my best friend replied.

"Maybe," I said dubiously. "But what does it mean?"

"Praise the Lord." Josh sounded mystified by my ignorance. "Just about everybody at my church uses it. They sign off chat or emails all the time with 'PTL'."

"That seems kind of … impious," Megan chided. "I mean, these are the same people that get on my case if I write 'Xmas' instead of 'Christmas,' no?"

"Yeah, whatever," Stuart said. "Why did a couple of Jesus freaks just come over and tell us that Jesus loves us?"

Again it was Megan who provided the voice of reason. "I think it's because they see Timothy as the antichrist."

I'd been called many things in my fourteen years, but this was the first time anyone had referred to me as the antichrist. And this from my girlfriend-to-be!

Talk of the antichrist clearly was not foreign to Josh, who, after all, attended a radically evangelical church. "No, I don't think they think that," he said in all seriousness. "If they did, they wouldn't have come and told us."

"Just burned a cross on your lawn," Lamont said.

I wasn't sure whether Lamont was joking, but I found the thought pretty scary, especially when Josh, our resident expert on fundamentalism, nodded in agreement. I tuned out most of the remaining lunch period and passed the rest of the school day quietly. I couldn't wait to get home and hear Mother's report on her meeting with Mr. Powers and Mrs. Barker.

Chapter 16

Surprises

When I got home, the only signs of life were the droning of a chant emanating from Goth Girl's room and a flashing red light on the answering machine in the kitchen. I listened to the messages, five in all, while I toasted and tucked into a blueberry Pop-Tart™. The first was a fascinating sales pitch for sump pump replacement, the second Grandma announcing a visit "next Sunday." Even as I wrote a note to my parents about Grandma coming, I wondered whether "next Sunday" referred to the very next Sunday or the following one, as in "next week Sunday." I supposed I would find out soon enough.

Message number 3 was for "Mandy," a slightly cryptic request from an unnamed person of ambiguous gender to attend a Toxic Paste concert "this coming Friday." As peculiar as I found GG's friends—I hadn't actually known that she had any—I was pleased that they could at least be precise about scheduling. I made a mental note to tell "Mandy" about her date, already looking forward to the opportunity to tell someone about my day. At least I knew GG wouldn't interrupt me.

Messages number 4 and 5 were from Dad and Mother respectively. Dad had called to give microwaving instructions for some frozen chicken fricassee—tonight was his night for giving citizenship lessons to Hmong women—and Mother had called to say she was heading back to the office to prepare the suit against my school. That news, plus the time stamp of her message—3:17—led me to believe the meeting hadn't gone so well.

I dearly hoped that my mother hadn't ruined my newly found rapport with my biology teacher and the principal of my school. Certainly my near future depended on it. My impression of Mrs. Barker had been that she was willing to see a potential lawsuit sportingly, but I had no idea how Mr. Powers would react. Yet the deed was done, so I saw no use fretting. I decided to deliver "Mandy's" message. If her mood was favorable, she just might sit still and look in my general direction while I held a monologue about my day. I really needed somebody to talk to.

I went upstairs to Goth Girl's room. I was just about to knock when I detected the most disturbing noises coming from her room—and I'm not referring to the recorded chanting, which I had come to think of as soothing. No, the sounds I am referring to were of an entirely different nature. I realize, of course, that at least some readers, their minds ever in the gutter, will now be thinking of the sorts of sounds generally associated with sex.

Shocking though it may be to some, I am intimately familiar with the sounds of sexual encounter. And if you have been paying attention, you will know why: my room is situated immediately adjacent to my parents' bedroom. So I was able to ascertain with some degree of certainty that the sounds I heard inside Goth Girl's room were not caused by people sharing carnal knowledge and pleasure, but were instead simple laughter.

While the image of my sister and a friend laughing was far less disturbing to my young, impressionable self than the thought of finding her, say, handcuffed to the bed or suspended from a sling, it seemed far less likely, given that I had heard my sister speak but once in the last few months. I knocked gently on the door. There was no response.

> [Aside: Lest you should think I have been consuming debauched DVDs, magazines or illicitly found websites, I should like to point out that both ideas—the handcuffs and the sling—come from prime-time television. The average teen is more likely to know about all manner of sexual practices than about how babies are made, which may account for our country's high rate of teenage pregnancy.]

I knocked again, a bit harder this time. The laughter and—dare I say it?—conversation stopped, and a few seconds later the door was opened. Through the tiny crack GG blocked with her massive body, all I was able to see was a black-booted foot that did not belong to her, perched behind her desk. I gave her the message, and the lifeless mien she presented communicated: a) that she had understood the message, b) that she was more than a little annoyed that I'd disturbed her and her company, and c) that if ever I dared to tell our parents what I had witnessed, I was dead meat. Such is the closeness of siblings that so much can be communicated with so little.

I withdrew quietly but unsatisfied: I still felt the need to unburden my soul, to communicate with another human being. It was only then that I realized that, although I had a best school friend, I didn't have anyone near where I lived who I was close to. Then I remembered Mike Petersson. He lived in the neighborhood and had expressed interest in hanging out sometime. I gave him a call.

"Hey, Timmy, that's a surprise," he said even before I could identify myself. I hate caller ID.

I reminded him that he'd suggested we hang out, and he immediately invited me over. "I have to finish my weight training and take a shower, so just let yourself in. My room is upstairs, the last one on the left."

I arrived at the Petersson abode around 20 minutes later and did as bidden. While waiting in Mike's room, I sat at his desk and looked around his room, which was decorated with posters of top athletes in just about every sport I could name. Even his screen saver showed Cristiano Ronaldo. Where I had shelves of books, Mike had display cases of trophies and racks for sporting equipment. The two of us obviously lead very different lives, I thought, and wondered whether Mike was really the right person to talk to given the mood I was in.

Mike entered the room wearing nothing but a towel, which looked way too small on his massive body. Unlike me, he didn't seem embarrassed by the situation, which I supposed had to do with him spending so much time in locker rooms. He pulled on a pair of shorts while I studied a wrestling trophy, and when I saw out of the corner of my eye that he was wearing a T-shirt, I again looked directly at him. Mike smiled and said, "So, what's up, Timmy?"

"Nothing special, why?"

"Well, on the phone you sounded like you wanted to talk." Mike was obviously more perceptive than I'd been willing to give him credit for, but I couldn't help but think the story I had to tell was probably beyond his grasp.

The big jock noted my hesitation and said, "Why don't we go outside and shoot some hoops? Maybe I can give you a few pointers."

"Yeah," I said, genuinely relieved to be doing something of a physical nature, as I'd come here without much of a plan. "Good idea."

"And who knows," Mike laughed, "maybe shooting hoops will loosen your tongue."

And it did.

Mike went easy on me, but to his credit, he didn't let me win at one-on-one. We played in short bursts, and as I caught my breath after each burst, I told him the short version of what was on my mind.

"Evolution," he said pensively. "That's apes and shit, right?"

"Yeah, that's right," I said, and I dashed left to shoot, nearly falling and looking terribly undignified in the process. But Mike didn't laugh the way the boys in gym always did when I made a fool of myself.

"You're not anticipating your moves, Tim," he said. I felt guilty for being surprised that he should use such a big word. "You have to shift your weight *before* you try and go for a rush like that. Here, watch me."

He stood in exactly the position I'd been in before my attempt at bluffing him. "Now this is what you just did. Your weight was here," he said, slapping his right leg, "so when you tried to move left, you almost fell." He demonstrated, falling dramatically and finishing with a double-somersault.

Mike picked himself up and brushed himself off, laughing along with me at his own dramatics. "Think one step ahead. Shift your weight before you go for it. But try and be all subtle-like so your opponent don't see—sorry, doesn't see—where you're going."

I found it endearing that Mike was trying to polish his grammar for my benefit, but it really wasn't necessary. And he was helping me in more ways than one: thinking a step ahead and not letting your opponent know what you're planning seemed like good advice, not only for basketball.

Mike proceeded to cream me on the driveway basketball court, and while I sat on the grass rubbing my scrawny and already sore legs, he went inside to get a couple of cans of soda. He tossed me one, and

I downed half of its contents within seconds. When I gave a muffled burp, Mike laughed. "So, Timothy Thompson is human—who knew?"

"What makes you say that, Mikey?"

"Oh, it's just—you seem so perfect, that's all. Like, you know everything. Me? I'm just a dumb jock."

"No, you're not, and no, I don't—know everything, I mean. You've been teaching me stuff since I got here. We just know different things, that's all."

"Yeah, I guess. Thing is, I'm doing 9th grade for the third time, and I'm still not getting it. Coach Braun says I gotta apply myself or he can't keep me on the team."

Mike looked so distraught sitting there on the grass next to me. "Maybe I can tutor you," I offered.

Mike seemed to perk up for a millisecond, but he sank into himself again almost immediately. "Nah, you'd be wasting your time."

"I know everything, remember?"

He smiled. "You'd do that?"

"I'd be happy to," I said, and I really meant it. I didn't have many friends, and I'd had a good time at Mike's place.

"OK, let's give it a try," Mike said. Then, after a few seconds, "You know, I been thinking about your problem with Mrs. Barker."

"You have?"

"Yeah. I was thinking—if Mrs. Barker won't teach evolution, why don't you? You're smart."

While I found the idea flattering—even intriguing—I recognized my limitations well enough to know I'm not a teacher. Tutoring Mike was one thing, but teaching a class? And there was no guarantee that Mrs. Barker would set aside time to let someone else teach something she didn't believe in. This idea of Mike's was no good.

"I don't think so, Mike. I'm not a teacher. And I don't know enough about the subject to teach it."

"Yeah, it's probably a dumb idea. I just thought that you and your brainiac friends could maybe do it."

"Hmm, maybe," I said. Mike was right—I wouldn't have to do it alone. And this would be a better Science Club project than a combat robot. "In fact, I'm starting to like your idea."

Mike the gentle giant beamed. I don't think he got a lot of compliments for his ideas.

I looked at my watch and was surprised to see that it was after eight. I hadn't even noticed that we'd been playing—and then sitting— under a floodlight.

Mike saw me look at my watch and asked, "You gotta go? 'Cause I was just gonna ask you to stay for supper. My mom'll be home from work in a few minutes, and she's bringing fried chicken."

"Thanks, Mike, but I should really be getting home." I knew no one would be there to expect me, and fried chicken with Mike and his mom sounded better than microwaved chicken fricassee by myself, but I wanted to get started on putting Mike's idea into action. Leaving was even more difficult when Mrs. Petersson pulled into the driveway and got out of her car with a steaming bucket of finger-lickin' good™ chicken.

Still, I said my good-byes and headed home, deep in thought. How could the Science Club compensate for Mrs. Barker's refusal to teach real biology? Could I convince the others that that would be more worthwhile than building a robot-killing robot? Would I be able to help Mike so he didn't get kicked off the football team? Where was his dad? Was my mother really going to sue my school? And whose black boot did I see in my sister's room earlier?

Chapter 17

Friends And Lovers

The next few days, things started to fall into place, and some of my questions were answered.

My mother's meeting with Principal Powers and Mrs. Barker had been cordial, she told me, but it hadn't brought about the results we'd hoped for. Mrs. Barker wasn't willing to teach evolution without introducing intelligent design as an alternative, which Mother, of course, was unwilling to accept. (After all, she had the law on her side here.) Mr. Powers had been extremely uncomfortable throughout the meeting. He was no friend of conflict, and he didn't appreciate being put in a situation in which he had to take sides. In the end, he felt he could not force Mrs. Barker to teach evolution, although he seemed highly concerned that the state teaching standards were not being met.

The very next day Mother filed for an injunction which would have forced the school district to comply with our wishes immediately until such time that a trial took place to decide the issue once and for all—or rather until appeal. The injunction was denied.

"This whole thing could take years," she lamented, "and meanwhile your class will continue to be ignorant."

I resented Mother's characterization of my AP biology fellows as ignorant, but her heart was in the right place.

"I never really expected to get the injunction, though," she said.

"Then why did you apply for it?" I asked naively.

Her response wasn't exactly an explanation: "It's all part of the game, Timothy."

I wasn't sure whether the remark was meant to indicate that Mother didn't want me to pursue the topic further, so, despite my curiosity about this mysterious thing called the law, I left it alone. Besides, I had news to share.

"On another note, the Science Club may have a solution for the 'ignorance' problem." I hoped Mother heard the quotation marks around the word *ignorance* and realized that I was miffed. "We're having a lecture series on evolution."

"What a good idea."

"It wasn't my idea; it was Mike Petersson's. But I convinced the Science Club to go along with it."

"Mike Petersson?" Mother said incredulously. "Isn't that the football player from Whitnall Avenue?"

"Yes, why?"

"Oh nothing. I just wouldn't have pegged him as the lecture series type."

Mother didn't realize how right she was. I'd already had my first tutoring session with Mike and had come to the conclusion that he was quite possibly right: he *was* just a dumb jock. I wasn't ready to give up on him though, especially since helping him with the material was honing my teaching skills, which I would be needing for my part in the lecture series. Besides, I was enjoying the time with Mike, him being the first friend I'd ever had outside my usual nerdy circle.

In the meantime, Josh was acting very strange. He'd been my best friend at school since the first day of junior high school. It was one of those things: one nerd recognized another, and we naturally gravitated toward each other. Although I would call us very close, in the slightly more than two years we had known each other, we had only met outside school once. This was mainly a logistical problem.

Josh and I live on opposite ends of the school district, and neither one of us has a "soccer mom"—or "soccer dad," for that matter. Our family has two cars, but my mother works long hours, and when my dad isn't running the household or making money buying and selling stock options on the Internet, he is usually volunteering for some cause or another. Josh's parents have one rather old and dilapidated pickup, and with four jobs and four children between them, they don't have time to chauffeur their kids around either.

The fact that Josh and I couldn't meet was never a problem; after all, we saw each other in school five days a week, texted or chatted almost every evening and talked on the phone a few times a week. Somewhat oddly, this only went on while school was in session. At the end of the last two school years, we said our good-byes and promised to stay in touch, but for some reason, we never did. Comprehensible or not, this was the dynamic of our friendship, and until recently, neither of us had seen fit to call it into question.

It all started at the Science Club meeting right after my mother's appointment with Mr. Powers and Mrs. Barker. As the attentive reader will recall, I intended to use that meeting to reverse the Club's decision to build a combat robot in favor of conducting a lecture series on evolution. When I first brought up the idea, the group was split down the middle, and Josh, to my dismay, was on the side of the fighting robots. Megan, to her credit, was with me.

Discussion went on for quite some time, and it appeared that more and more club members were coming around to my way of thinking, i.e. that educating our fellow students and fighting the forces of ignorance were more important than devising a digital device of demonic destruction. After the longest discussion Mr. Grass could remember ever hearing in Science Club, Josh was the last holdout for the robot. It took him a while to realize that he was the only one still arguing, at which point he finally caved.

"Well, I can see I'm the only one who thinks it's important to stick with a decision once it's made. So fine, go ahead: have the lecture series for all I care." He folded his arms across his chest and tuned us out for the remainder of the meeting.

We didn't go on much longer, as it was getting late, but we agreed that we'd all come with ideas for presentations and lectures to discuss the following week. All except Josh, of course, who was still moping.

On the way out I signaled to Megan that I wanted to be alone with Josh. I had asked her before if I could walk part of the way home with her—until our paths parted—and she had agreed! But fortunately Megan seemed to understand instinctively that I needed instead to placate my pouting pal.

Josh was making it extremely difficult to walk with him by alternately walking slowly and quickly, making sudden stops to inspect bulletin boards and even lockers in the hall along the way. When he had to accept that he wasn't going to be able to shake me, he said, "Why aren't you with your girlfriend?"

So that's what this was about: Josh was jealous!

"You mean Megan?" I asked incredulously.

"Who else? Or do you have another girlfriend?"

"I don't even have one girlfriend, Josh. Not yet anyway."

He looked sullen, deep in thought. "Whatever."

"Josh, are you jealous? Of me and Megan?"

"No, of course not." My best friend looked distinctly uncomfortable. "Why would I be jealous?"

"Maybe *jealous* isn't the right word. It just sounded like you resented that I was spending time with Megan.—You're still my best friend, you know."

"Yeah?" Josh beamed at me.

"Yeah."

We walked together in silence for a short time. After this tender moment had passed, Josh suddenly said, "So, you wanna do one of the presentations together—you and me?"

I had been hoping to do something with Megan but thought it unwise to say so. "Sure, but I thought you weren't going to do anything. You weren't exactly in favor of this whole lecture series idea."

"I was never really *against* it. I just wanted to build a robot, that's all. But I don't wanna be a sore loser."

"What about your family? If we get up and do a presentation together, they're going to find out. And maybe your pastor too."

"Oh yeah. I hadn't thought of that. Maybe I could work behind the scenes; you can be the face of whatever it is we do."

"OK," I said. "That might work." Why not? I thought. I'm already the antichrist. And maybe Josh and I could work with Megan. Then he would see that she's not so bad, and that I can have a girlfriend *and* a best friend.

"Good," Josh said. "That settles it then.—Hey, if you have time now, we could start brainstorming some ideas for our lecture."

"No, sorry. I already have plans." And before Josh could get his knickers in a twist again, I made sure he knew I wasn't going to see Megan. "I have some tutoring to do."

"Really? Who are you tutoring?"

"Mike Petersson."

"The jock?"

"You know him?"

"Doesn't everybody?" Josh seemed almost insulted by my question. "He's the star of our football team."

I hadn't realized that Mike had star status. "Well, if I can't help him get his grades up, his football days will be over soon."

We arrived at Josh's locker—time to go our separate ways. "Well, good luck with the tutoring. The whole school is depending on you."

We said our good-byes, after which, thanks to Josh, I had to walk the entire way home by myself.

Chapter 18
Meeting Miss Abrams

Once we'd committed to doing the lecture series, I was forced to confront one of my worst fears.

This may seem unlikely, perhaps even shocking, but I, Timothy Thompson, a.k.a. Tim-Tom, one of the biggest nerds known to humankind, have been deathly afraid of libraries for most of my life. Whenever I have had to enter a library, especially a school library, I have dreams about it. They are not pleasant dreams, and they usually involve me not being able to find the catalogue, suddenly and inexplicably forgetting the alphabet, or wandering amongst the shelves naked while being whipped by a 70-something matron dressed as a dominatrix. (This last part of my dream was a late addition whose arrival corresponded roughly with the onset of puberty.)

As far as I know—and my memory goes back to age three, you will recall—there has never been any sort of incident that might have caused these irrational fears. I know that there is generally a sign above the catalogue, and that it is either a computer, or in old-style libraries, a large cabinet or set of cabinets; I have, since I learned my ABCs at the tender age of three, never once forgotten even part of the alphabet; and lastly, I have never been known to wander naked anywhere, much less in library stacks. And for the record, I have yet to encounter a dominatrix of any age; nor have I been whipped by one.

Whatever the reason for my phobia, I had little choice but to seek out Omar L. Batshit High School's library. There I found my worst fears not confirmed, but dashed. First of all, the librarian was young, I suspect in her early 20s. And she was pretty, in a wholesome kind of way, with a fine-featured, friendly face and yellow hair, which she wore in a crew cut. Most of the boys at school think she's a dyke, which is a not-very-nice word for a lesbian. (The girls, as far as I know, have yet to weigh in on the subject.) I have no knowledge of her sexual orientation myself and will, therefore, refrain from comment. I would, however, like to say that if she is indeed a lesbian—or in fact transgender, as another common schoolyard theory would have it—I wholly support her right to live and love as she pleases. But I digress.

Miss Abrams was, like me, new at Batshit High, and she had just begun the process of converting one end of the room into a reading lounge. Although the library was a bit of a construction site, I immediately felt comfortable there. And Miss Abrams was most accommodating, offering help without making me feel in any way inadequate. Her small, wiry body and short-cropped hair made her look tough, but not in a whipping dominatrix kind of way. To the contrary, the warm and genuine smile on her bright face told me I needn't feel intimidated by her. I trusted this woman without hesitation and confessed my ignorance, albeit indirectly.

"This is my first visit, and I wonder whether you couldn't show me around?"

"I'd be happy to," she said, offering me her hand to shake. "I'm Emily Abrams, by the way."

"Timothy Thompson. Pleased to meet you, Ms. Abrams."

"It's Miss," she corrected, then proceeded to show me the catalogue, explain the arrangement of the shelves and tell me about her plans for the reading lounge. The tour was enlightening, and I am pleased to report that I haven't had a library nightmare since.

"So tell me, Timothy," Miss Abrams segued from her presentation, "what brings you here today?"

"Well, I was hoping to find some books on evolution."

"Science is right here," she said and led the way.

Most of the books I found on my subject were ancient. Opening the first, a copy of Darwin's *On the Origin of Species*, I fully expected to find a personal dedication from the author himself. What I found instead shocked both me and Miss Abrams: the book was scrawled with obscenities, and someone had gone to a great deal of trouble to write the word "Lies" in a pseudo-Gothic script diagonally across every right-hand page.

"Somebody had a lot of time on his or her hands," I remarked.

"That's for sure," Miss Abrams said breezily, taking the book. "It's probably best if I replace this one with an e-book. At least that can't be defaced."

I didn't reveal that I had figured out months before how to hack most e-books, as I doubted that anyone smart enough to do so would use the knowledge to deface Darwin. "Good idea," I said, reaching for the other books on evolution. All of them had been written in, though none as badly as the book by the blasphemous *Beagle* biologist.

"Just tell me which books you need, Timothy, and I'll replace them as fast as possible."

"What I really need," I told her, "is a book or two that explain the controversy between evolution and intelligent design slash creationism."

"So you're the one!" Miss Abrams seemed delighted, as if meeting a celebrity. "I heard about your run-in with Mrs. Barker. That *was* you, wasn't it?"

I felt my face flush red as I admitted to being the infamous student who had crossed swords with his biology teacher. When she asked me for "all the gory details," I filled her in on our plans for a lecture series.

"That's terrific," she said. "I can help you with presentation tools as well as background materials. And if you like, I could put you in touch with a possible guest speaker."

"Guest speaker?" I hadn't thought of the possibility up to that point.

"Sure. He teaches chemical biology at Northwestern, and he's a very good speaker. I'm sure he'd be willing to come here for a guest lecture."

"I don't know, Miss Abrams. A college professor?"

Miss Abrams understood my hesitation and assured me, "Oh, don't worry. He knows how to tone down the science-speak for a lay audience."

"We couldn't pay him."

"Don't worry about that either," Miss Abrams said. "I'm sure he'd be happy to do it for free. He's kind of a missionary when it comes to evolution, and if I ask him nicely, I'm sure he'll do it."

Catching the dubious look on my face, she added, almost embarrassed, "He's my dad."

I instantly made the connection. "Cyrus Abrams is your father? He's practically my hero."

"Mine too," the proud daughter beamed. "So do you want me to ask him?"

"I have to check with the other members of the Science Club first, but yes! I'd love to have him."

"OK, just let me know. Now, let's make a list of what you're going to need."

The chance of meeting one of the world's foremost experts on evolutionary biology had me pretty excited, so when I got home that evening, I sent an email to Mr. Grass and everyone in the Science Club. The response was enthusiastic, to put it mildly; only Mr. Grass registered doubt, but that had more to do with school board policy on guest speakers that would require a mountain of red tape on his part. I was confident that we could convince him and that we would put on the most amazing lecture series ever. No one, I sincerely believed, would come out of our lectures with any doubt as to the veracity of evolution and the superiority of the scientific method.

Yes, this seemed like what was perhaps the most exciting day of my life. It was also the day when things started to go really wrong.

Chapter 19

Sources

I only later learned that it was Mr. Powers who managed to negotiate all the hoops that were required to get school board approval of a guest speaker for our lecture series. Apparently overwhelming opinion in the superintendent's office was that it would be wiser to avoid controversy by keeping something as "divisive" as evolution out of our schools, and there was an effort to suppress the lecture series altogether.

My sources tell me that our principal made quite a forceful case, using mainly the state learning standards as his argument. For all the man's reluctance to abide disagreement within his school, he was a formidable "extramural" (to use one of his favorite words) advocate for our cause. I do admire the man.

In the weeks that followed, I had ample opportunity to get to know our principal better. Not that I was sent there again by an angry teacher! Instead, Mr. Powers "requested the pleasure of [my] company," as he so quaintly put it, about once every two weeks.

The first time I was summoned to the principal's office, my trepidation was palpable, but Mrs. McDermitt assured me that all was well. Not that the infamous McDoormat actually spoke the words to me! No, it was the absence of meanness in her face that clued me in. Why then, I wondered, was I here?

I certainly didn't mind having an excuse to miss phy ed, even though Coach Braun had made it infinitely clear that he was not at all happy to allow me to escape his sadistic rituals. Still, I had to wonder what was going on.

That first non-disciplinary meeting with Principal Powers began innocuously: "Timothy, welcome. Please, have a seat."

Once I'd settled into the proffered armchair, Mr. Powers continued. "I can imagine you're curious as to why I should have invited you here this morning."

He intoned it as a question, so I answered. "Yes, sir."

The old man repressed a grin. I think my politeness and formality amused him. "I just wanted to make sure that everything is all right."

Why wouldn't everything be all right, I wondered. "Yes, Mr. Powers, everything is fine."

"Good, good," he said, but it sounded as if his mind was drifting. "So no one has caused you any harm—or threatened to?"

No more than usual, I thought, although this wasn't actually the case. Mr. Braun hadn't dared to repeat the dodgeball incident, but I had taken more than my share of elbows while shooting hoops when the coach "wasn't watching," and he seemed to take great pleasure using me to demonstrate what could happen on all variety of gymnastic equipment if something went wrong. My body was covered with bruises and abrasions, but I had no desire to show them to my principal or even to mention them to him. Nor did I want to bring up the "accidents" I was having in the halls, or the fact that three juniors had followed me half-way home the evening before, taunting me as "godless" and spitting on the back of my windbreaker.

"No sir. Why do you ask?"

"I have my sources, Timothy, I can assure you, and there has been some indication that you might be the victim of chicanery."

"Chicanery, sir? I'm afraid I don't know what that is."

"Chicanery? It's from the French, I believe, and it refers to trickery. Are people playing tricks on you, Timothy? Treating you badly?"

I hesitated perhaps a tad too long before answering "No, not at all," and Mr. Powers picked up on that.

"You're a good lad, Mr. Thompson, and it speaks to your character that you should put such a brave face on it. But please note: if the tomfoolery becomes intolerable—whether perpetrated by other students or by members of the faculty—I want to know about it. I won't have anyone intimidating one of my charges for making his opinion known or standing up for legitimate concerns."

"I understand, sir. Thank you."

Mr. Powers looked at his watch, which he pulled by its fob from a waistcoat pocket. "There isn't much point in you going to your physical education class any more, but I don't suppose that will be the cause of much chagrin on your part. And I'm sure you can make yourself useful in the library until the end of the period. Mrs. McDermitt will give you the appropriate pass."

And she did, the moment I left Mr. Powers' office.

I had found that first meeting with Mr. Powers quite extraordinary. How, I wondered, did he know that I was being "chicaned" by teachers and students—who were these "sources" he had referred to? Why had he taken such an interest in my fate? And how did Mrs. McDermitt know when I was ready to emerge from the office and what sort of pass to give me? I didn't like having so many questions and so few answers.

I went to the library as instructed, but Miss Abrams was busy doing an orientation with a group of special needs kids, so I couldn't make myself useful, as Mr. Powers had suggested. Instead I decided to use the time to read up on evolution. Somewhat surprisingly, a few of the books I'd asked Miss Abrams to order had already arrived; unsurprisingly, a copy of Cyrus Abrams' tome was also in stock. I buried my nose in it until the bell rang.

When I arrived at my AP biology class, Mrs. Barker smiled almost mischievously at me. "Did you and Principal Powers have a nice chat, Timothy?"

I tried not to betray my surprise at the degree to which she was informed of my comings and goings and simply responded, "Yes, we did."

"You'll no doubt be happy to hear that Mr. Powers is considering making attendance at your lecture series mandatory for everyone in this class."

"Really?" I said, somewhat incredulously. I hadn't even been aware that the lecture series plans were common knowledge, much less that Mr. Powers was planning to promote it to the level of course material.

"Yes, indeed," Mrs. Barker said cheerily. "And I'm looking forward to a fruitful discussion with Cyrus Abrams. He wouldn't happen to be related to our Miss Emily Abrams, would he?"

Mrs. Barker seemed to know an awful lot about the Science Club's plans. I didn't want to be caught in a lie, so I avoided the issue. "It's probably best if you ask her, Mrs. Barker."

"Oh, it's not really that important. Do sit down, Timothy. I have a class to teach."

Instead of following Mrs. Barker's lecture on invertebrates, I pondered the events of that morning. Who were Principal Powers' mysterious "sources"? Was Mrs. McDermitt listening in on conversations in Mr. Powers' office? If so, was Mr. Powers aware of her snooping? How did Mrs. Barker know so much about our Science Club's plans?

Going beyond that morning, I contemplated Coach Braun's campaign of torture and humiliation; was it somehow connected to this whole sordid affair, to my being labeled the antichrist? For that matter, who was spreading the word among the student body about my involvement in a science v. religion controversy? How did the couple who appeared at our lunch table to tell me that God loves me know that there might be doubt on that front? How did the junior spitters who had followed me home get their (mis)information—who had told them that I was "godless"?

Indeed, what was going on at my school? Was there some sort of Christian conspiracy, or at the very least a network of evangelicals acting against me? Or was I simply paranoid? This last thought was where I'd arrived by the time the bell interrupted my biology class musings.

Paranoid was a diagnosis I could deal with, as it required no further thought or action on my part. If I was simply being paranoid, I could dismiss further reflections on the Christian conspiracy theory, relegating it to an inactive portion of my brain. And that's what I did for the rest of the day, and for several days after that, until events once again forced these thoughts to the fore.

Chapter 20

Tim-Tom, Secret Muslim

After deciding that any feelings of persecution I was having were the product of an over-active imagination, I felt infinitely better. I was now able to shrug off Coach Braun's meanness, Mrs. Barker's sugary sweetness, and the bullies' general nastiness. All a coincidence, I told myself. Simply the result of being a runty little geek in a school system that values the jockstrap over the pocket protector. (Not that I myself use pocket protectors! I confess, however, that I do perhaps spend an inordinate amount of time with those who do.) None of this, I had convinced myself, had anything at all to do with my assertion of First Amendment rights or the lecture series I was helping to plan.

Life was definitely easier without the paranoia, and I was able to maintain my devil-may-care attitude toward all things threatening for nearly a week. Then one afternoon during Ms. Pewney's English class, a note landed on my desk. And I do quite literally mean "landed," as the many-times-folded piece of paper seemed to fall from directly above me onto my open copy of *The Complete Works of William Shakespeare*.

I let out a small, startled sound which caused Ms. Pewney to stop writing on the board and turn toward the class.

"Did you have a question, Timothy?" she asked, apparently somewhat perplexed that I, of all her students, should disrupt the proceedings.

"No, I'm sorry, Ms. Pewney," I answered, trying to sound reflective. "I just had a realization, that's all."

"Would you care to share it with the rest of us?"

Ever the quick thinker, I recalled something I'd read about the character Mercutio in *Romeo and Juliet*, which we were reading. "Well," I hesitated, "it's not exactly mind-boggling, and I don't know why I didn't pick up on it sooner. The name 'Mercutio' is probably related to the word 'mercurial,' which describes his impulsiveness pretty much to a T. The Bard probably chose the name accordingly."

"An excellent observation, Timothy," Ms. Pewney enthused. "If Mercutio hadn't been, as you say, mercurial, he wouldn't have had to die. That wouldn't have made much of a play, though."

Ms. Pewney went on to explain that Mercutio wasn't, as I'd claimed, an invention of Shakespeare's, but had already been a character in the sources Shakespeare had used when he wrote his play. As she elaborated on the whole sources thing, I wondered whether this was to be one of those occasions when my fellow students would be grateful for my having got the teacher off track so their minds could wander, or if I would be feeling the slings and arrows of their outrageous derision (with apologies to Shakespeare for mangling the quote from *Hamlet,* Act 3, Scene 1) as soon as the class ended.

Then alas, the bell signaling the end of the sixth and final period of the day rang, and we all gathered up our things to head on home or to extra-curriculars. Among the effects on my desk was the folded note, which I discreetly stuffed into the pocket of my jeans. As I was on my way out, Ms. Pewney asked me, "So what did the note say?"

"Note? What note?" Prevaricate, Timothy!

"The one that caused you to squeak while I was writing on the board," she smiled benevolently. "Nice save, by the way."

"What do you mean by 'save,' Ms. Pewney?" I asked, as I genuinely did not understand.

"Your remarks on the name and character Mercutio, of course. You're very quick on your feet, aren't you? Most teachers probably wouldn't have caught the bluff."

I felt exposed, as if I'd forgotten to put on pants that morning, and now suddenly found myself in front of this woman with only my tighty-whities between her and my most private of parts. I decided that the best riposte was a compliment, as indeed her observations had, in a way, been worthy of same. "You are very observant, Ms. Pewney." I gave her my best attempt at a coy look as I said this.

"Thank you." I must have pulled off the coy look, as she responded in kind. "So what was in the note?"

There was obviously no fooling this woman, and it was clear to me that any attempt to distract her was doomed to failure. I produced the note, which I myself had yet to see, from my pocket. "I haven't read it, Ms. Pewney," I said, stating the obvious, and began to unfold the mysterious missive.

Inside was a primitive drawing of a person, meant to be me, wearing a turban. The caption beneath the drawing read "Osama Tim Laden." A moment passed before I realized that my mouth was hanging open, making me look rather like my jaw-challenged friend Stuart. I closed it and started to wonder whether now was the right time to be paranoid again.

I felt Ms. Pewney staring at me while I pored over the drawing, yet I continued to study it. As I noted above, the style was primitive, a fact that was amplified by the lettering, which looked as if it had been executed by a five-year-old holding a crayon in his fist. What I hadn't noticed at first was the circle drawn around the figure's (i.e. my) head, with a vertical and a horizontal line across the diameter. In case that description isn't clear to you, think crosshairs. Think rifle scope. Think of what happened to Osama bin (not Tim) Laden. (In case you have been living on another planet, bin Laden was the terrorist ultimately responsible for the 9/11 attacks on New York, Washington, D.C., and an innocuous field near Shanksville, Pennsylvania. American Special Forces shot him in the head almost ten years later.)

Suddenly I was feeling paranoid and the need to talk to Dr. Feelgood.

Before I could get lost in my reverie, Ms. Pewney spoke. "You know what I find most disturbing?"

"The not-so-veiled threat to my life?"

"Well, that too. But I meant the paper—and of course the fact that it's a photocopy."

"Oh shit!" slipped out of me before I could stop it. "Sorry, Ms. Pewney. I didn't mean to …" Our school has a zero-tolerance policy on swearing, so I was concerned that I might not only be killed by some mad student with very poor drawing skills, but that I could be suspended. But reporting my indiscretion was far from my English teacher's mind.

"Oh, don't worry. Your rather mild expletive is nothing compared to what I thought when *I* saw the drawing," she surprised me. Her regal bearing had made me think she would be averse to using any form of curse.

"Thank you," I said, relieved. "So you're saying … there are more of these?" I was examining the note to confirm that it was indeed a photocopy. "But what did you mean about the paper?"

"That's school paper," she said. "That copy was produced here."

"Not wishing to be contrary, Ms. Pewney, but it's just paper. I mean, how can you tell?"

"That low grade of paper comes from the superintendent's office. They buy it in bulk. No one else uses that junk. I don't know how many times I've complained to Principal Powers about it."

Now that she had pointed it out, I could see what she meant. The paper was thinner than any other I'd ever held, and it definitely wasn't white. In fact, on closer inspection I could see that the color varied somewhat from top to bottom. "Hmm, I see what you mean. Maybe we could have a fund-raising drive of some kind and buy decent paper. I'd be happy to help out."

She smiled sympathetically. "At the minute I think we have more pressing problems than the paper. Someone is making threats against you. I think we need to speak with Mr. Powers immediately."

I stole a glance at my watch, but she caught it. "Or we could do it in the morning. You obviously have someplace to go."

I flashed a sheepish grin. "I'm meeting with someone from Science Club about our lecture series, and after that I have some tutoring to do."

"Really?" She sounded impressed. "Who are you tutoring, if I may ask?"

"Of course. It's Mike Petersson."

"Interesting. I know Mike; he's in one of my English classes." I'd known that because Mike had told me he had remedial English with her. "Keep up the good work then. He's been showing improvement lately."

Ms. Pewney and I said our good-byes. That was my first encounter with the woman outside our lessons, and I really liked her—even if I did find it unnerving standing close to her, because of her imposing height.

After leaving Ms. Pewney's room, I dashed straight to my meeting with Josh to work on the slides for our multimedia presentation. I didn't even bother going to my locker first, for I was late and worried that Josh might give up on me. I wasn't normally late for anything.

Josh was just packing up his stuff when I arrived, out of breath, in the science room. "Hey," he said, "I was getting worried about you."

"Come on, Josh," I protested. "It's only a few minutes."

"Well, I thought you were dead." To underscore the drama of this statement, he held up a copy of the Osama Tim Laden poster.

"Where'd you get that?" I asked apprehensively.

"They're all over the school, Timothy. Don't tell me you didn't see any on the way here. Unless I got them all…" He pointed to a small pile of the papers that he had torn down.

"Hey, thanks, man," I said, patting his shoulder bro-style. My friend looked as if he was about to cry, so I decided some jesting was in order. "Not a very good likeness, is it?"

"You jerk," he sputtered and punched me in the left biceps, or what passes as biceps on my scrawny frame. "This is serious, Timothy. Someone is threatening you."

"Yeah, I know," I said sullenly. "But they're just trying to scare us."

"Well, they're doing a pretty good job!"

Josh and I went on like this for another twenty minutes. Once we realized we weren't going to get any work done, we gave up for the day and went our separate ways. As I was walking to my locker, I saw and removed two of the Osama posters. I was concerned what I might find on or in my locker when I got there, but there were no posters, and no booby traps.

I made it home without incident, dropped off my books and went to Mike's house, hoping against hope that football practice would have let out early and that he'd be there. He wasn't. I was about to plop myself down at a picnic table in the Peterssons' back yard when I saw Mike's basketball. Though it was somewhat out of character for me, I picked up the ball and started shooting hoops.

I don't know how long I was at it, but time seemed to pass very quickly while I was moving around the court. It was all quite therapeutic. By the time I heard Mike calling my name, I had worked up quite a sweat.

"You looked pretty good there, Tim. You're improving."

I found this compliment strangely gratifying. It made me want to report what Ms. Pewney had told me about his progress, but I thought better of it: I wouldn't want Mike to think I was talking to his teachers about him. Instead I just said, "Thanks. You wanna get to work?"

Mike hesitated ever so slightly before saying, "Sure." I decided to ask him about it.

"Yeah," he said slowly, "I wanted to ask you something."

"OK, ask away!" I said breezily.

"How come you didn't tell me you're a muslin?"

It took me a moment to realize that he thought I was of the Islamic faith, not a piece of cloth. "You mean Muslim."

"So it's true?"

"That I'm a Muslim? No. Where did you get that anyway?"

"It was after practice tonight in the locker room. Some of the guys were talkin'."

"About me? What were they saying?"

"Oh, that you're a Muslim and that's why you're doin' that stuff against the Christians." He paused for a moment. "Muslim—that's like a terrorist, right?"

"No," I said emphatically. "Come on, let's shoot some hoops, and I'll explain."

It hadn't taken long for me to realize that Mike could take in a lot more information when he was moving. Sitting and studying in his room, as we did on rainy days, he had the attention span of a ruta-baga, but walking or on the basketball court, he seemed to soak up information. (OK, I exaggerate...) Within twenty minutes, Mike had a fairly firm grasp on the tenets of Islam, the reasons for the association many people have between Muslims and terrorists, and why believing in evolution isn't doing anything against Christians. And by the time we'd finished, he also knew that muslin was a kind of cotton cloth and misused the word to mean "Muslim" in a mere 15% of occurrences.

I, for my part, also had a pretty firm grasp on what was going on at school. People were trying to discredit me by playing on negative stereotypes about Muslims so that what I had to say about evolution and creationism would hold less credence. Meanwhile, my tutoring technique was improving my balance and aim, and I was starting to appreciate physical activity for the first time in my life. Yes, tutoring was definitely good for both tutor and tutee.

As Mike and I said our good-byes, Mike reminded me of something I'd long set aside. "Oh, by the way… Mrs. Barker gave us the permission slips for the science field trip. It says where we're going. Nothing about a creation museum."

"That's good," I said. "So where is she taking you?"

Mike pulled a crumpled and somewhat sweaty piece of paper out of his back pocket. "I knew you'd wanna know, so I brought it with me," he said proudly. "Here," he pointed, and handed me the paper.

No, there was no mention of a creation museum. In fact, the itinerary included "a natural history museum" in—you guessed it— Petersburg, Kentucky. I felt perfectly reasonable in my assumption that there was no other "natural history" museum in Petersburg than the infamous Creation Museum, the one where "children play and dinosaurs roam." I knew Mike was looking forward to getting away, so I didn't let on that I was going to do everything in my power to see to it that this field trip didn't take place.

Chapter 21

Oy Vey, Now I'm Jewish?

That Wednesday we had our usual family dinner event. I was the last to arrive, two and one half minutes after the appointed time. Mother was not amused.

"Dinner is at eight," she said before I even managed to sit down or offer my apologies for my late arrival. "You know how important these meals are for the continued functioning of our family unit."

I could have said so much at that juncture: that those were Dr. Feelgood's words coming out of Mother's mouth, or that there could be no talk of "continued" functioning of our family unit, as that would imply that there was a functioning unit to continue in the first place. I might also have explained why I was late. Instead I said, "I'm sorry, Mother. It won't happen again."

"Apology accepted, Timothy. Now, shall we start enjoying the delightful meal your father has prepared for us?"

And delightful it was, even though the word "delightful" does not normally feature prominently in my active vocabulary. There were game hens (which, by the way, are neither game nor necessarily hens) roasted with garlic and rosemary, green beans bundled and wrapped in bacon and a marbled mash of sweet and regular potatoes. The game hen was in fact so delightful that Goth Girl actually reacted to her first bite with an audible "Mmm," causing us all to stare and her to turn a very pale shade of pink.

This behavior was actually consistent with certain other signs of late that my sister was, in fact, human. I had only a few days earlier seen her eyes focus—if only for a brief moment—on an egg. And when she and I crossed paths in the hallway, I thought I detected recognition on her face. The façade was cracking, if in geological time, and I chalked it up to the black-booted person I was hearing with increasing frequency in her room in the afternoons. I had yet to discern whether the person was of the male or female persuasion or what the nature of their visits were, but they seemed to be having an effect on "Mandy."

Mother provided the second surprise of the evening when she didn't ask us about our weeks, but dived right into a report of her own. "I had an interesting phone call this afternoon," she began without any sort of introduction or segue. "It was a reporter."

"Hey, that's great, Ronnie," Dad said. "Another feature on the Midwest's premiere lawyer?"

"No, but thank you for that," Mother replied. "It was about our suit against the school district."

Mother looked at me pointedly as she said this. Again I was feeling rebuke where none was deserved.

"I had nothing to do with it, Mother," I protested.

"Apparently inviting Cyrus Abrams to your lecture series has attracted some attention."

"OK…" I said hesitantly, "but how is that a bad thing?"

"Did I say it was?" Mother tucked into her game hen. "Mmm, this is excellent, Paul. I do believe you've outdone yourself."

After a moment's pondering, I was still confused. The look Mother had cast me had been unmistakably castigating. There was obviously more to this tale. But what?

"Anyway," Mother suddenly continued, "this reporter told me that our case has moved ahead. Apparently Judge Harris has decided to handle it as a priority after all."

Again Mother looked at me accusingly, and I hadn't the faintest clue why.

"It was rather embarrassing that I had to find this out from a reporter," Mother said, and again this didn't seem to be my fault. "I called Judge Harris's clerk and he confirmed that the case was being expedited. He hinted that someone had been putting pressure on the judge to move it up on her docket. The clerk also was mystified that I hadn't been notified, since the hearing is scheduled for next week Thursday, and he'd sent out the papers weeks ago.

"Slowly but surely I'm getting the impression that there are forces at work here that we know nothing about."

"You mean something supernatural?" I ventured.

Mother guffawed. "Not unless these cultists have invoked the Holy Ghost, Timothy. No, I think someone in the courthouse held those papers back deliberately—a sympathizer for the other side. Twenty minutes after I got off the phone with Judge Harris's office, the papers were delivered. And the time stamp from her clerk indicated that he'd been telling the truth: he *had* sent the case file three weeks ago."

"That's outrageous," Dad exclaimed. "They can't just go holding stuff back from you—that's illegal!"

"Yes, Paul, if we could prove it, somebody at the courthouse would be looking at serious jail time."

"Yeah," Dad had to admit, "it'll be impossible to prove it was done deliberately. But now there's documentation of when you got the file. You can use that to get a postponement, can't you? I mean, you'll need more time to prepare."

"Two problems with that. I've filed so many motions asking to expedite this thing, I'd look like a fickle bitch if I requested a postponement right before we go to trial."

"Yeah, that would look bad," Dad agreed. "What's the other problem?"

Mother drew a deep breath. "The other problem … is that we no longer have a case."

"What?!" Dad and I asked in unison. Even GG raised her head from its position just above her plate and pointed it in Mother's general direction.

Mother, meanwhile, was taking great pleasure in ignoring our inquiring stares as she ate heartily from her game hen. It was me who dared to interrupt.

"Mom, I don't get it. Why don't we have a case any more?"

"Well, Timothy," she said as she slowly turned toward me, "as *somebody* neglected to inform me, Mr. Powers has decided to require everyone in your biology class to attend the lecture series you're doing."

"Yes, but how does that affect our case?"

"Our case hinges on a state requirement that evolution has to be taught in public schools. Nowhere does it say that it has to be taught by the biology teacher."

"That sly old dog," Dad said with a mixture of annoyance and admiration in his voice. "I didn't think Powers had it in him."

"Wait, I'm confused," I said. "Are you saying we have to drop our lawsuit?"

"Possibly," Mother said contemplatively.

"I'm really sorry, Mother. I had no idea …"

"I know, Timothy," she said. "It's not your fault. I just wish you'd told me, that's all." She drew a deep breath. "Is there anything else I should know—anything at all?"

So I told her about everything: the bullying, my meetings with Principal Powers, the Osama Tim Laden posters. For some reason she found the posters humorous.

"I'm sorry for laughing, Timothy," Mother apologized between bouts of laughter. "I don't even know why I find it funny."

Mother's laughter, however unmotivated, proved contagious. Dad and I were soon in tears from laughing so hard, and I'm fairly sure I caught a crack of a smile on GG's face as well. As we were calming down and wiping the tears out of our eyes a few minutes later, we were shocked out of our seats by a crash from the living-room.

"What the ...?" Mother, Dad and I said in unison, while GG said nothing but looked suddenly alert. As Dad dashed into the living-room, I saw GG focus her eyes on him curiously, only to drift back into her catatonic state as soon as his frame was out the door.

"I don't believe it," we heard him say from the next room, and now deeming it safe, we followed him. Lying in a pile of glass that had only moments before been our front window was a sizable red brick.

"That brick didn't fly in here by itself," Dad said, his mind apparently as sharp as ever.

"It certainly didn't," Mother agreed, making me wonder why grown-ups so often demonstrate this penchant for stating the obvious.

"There's a note," a gruff, vaguely familiar voice said. It was my sister.

GG's sudden loquaciousness rendered my parents and me temporarily immobile, but we recovered relatively quickly.

"Should I look what it says?" I asked. "Or will the police want to dust it for prints?"

"You've been watching too much television, Timothy," Mother said drily. "The police won't bother with prints for a simple act of vandalism."

"Still …" I said, and took out my handkerchief, adroitly using it to cover my hands as I unwrapped the note and its rubber band from the brick. "The good news is that the brick looks like it came from next door."

Our neighbors were having a new garden path laid, and the brick I was holding was the same purplish color and glazed on one side, just like the bricks in the pile next door.

"How is that good news?" Dad wanted to know.

"It could suggest that this was a spontaneous deed," Mother answered before I could. "The perpetrator didn't bring the brick with him."

"But he brought this," I said, holding up a copy of the infamous Osama Tim Laden poster, onto which someone had scrawled with orange highlighter, "Die, Jew Boy!!!"

"This is serious," Dad said gravely. "That's a direct threat."

"I don't get it," I admitted. "How can I be a Jew *and* a secret Muslim? Doesn't one sort of rule out the other?"

"That's your problem, Timothy," Mother said. "You're so smart that you can't think like a stupid person. I'll explain it to you after I call the police."

The police actually came very quickly when my mother emphasized the threat over the act of vandalism, but Mother managed to enlighten me on the Jewish Muslim question.

"Jewish people have been the scapegoats for just about everything since Christ walked the earth. They've been taking the blame for killing Jesus for two thousand years, and although most of the established Christian denominations have let that go, the Fundamentalists haven't."

"But how can they say I'm Jewish and compare me to Osama bin Laden? Bin Laden wasn't a Jew."

"No, he was a Muslim—a bad Muslim, an evil Muslim, far out of the mainstream—but a Muslim. So, 'Muslim' has become the new scapegoat, and to the simple-minded, 'Jewish' and 'Muslim' become synonymous. Both terms simply mean 'bad,' and anybody who is against their brand of Christianity must be Jewish, Muslim, or both."

"Kind of like when the Tea Partiers called the president a fascist and a communist in the same breath?"

"Exactly like that," Mother affirmed. "But let's go back to the wonderful dinner your father cooked for us. Maybe we can at least finish the main course before the police get here."

Chapter 22
Satan Makes An Appearance

The court date came and went pretty much as Mother had predicted. She tried to argue a somewhat arcane point of law that would have allowed the case to proceed, but the judge dismissed the suit. I wasn't there, but apparently she decided that our lawsuit was "moot," since my biology class was to receive instruction in evolution, if not by our actual teacher.

Perhaps not surprisingly after the first member of the press had shown up to interview Mother, a gaggle of reporters was present for the all-too-brief hearing. The disappointment at the suit's dismissal was tangible in the short, well-hidden articles devoted to the subject. Only a single, self-described "progressive" website did an in-depth analysis of the issues involved, concluding that there would have been but one possible outcome had the case been tried: the judge would have had to order Mrs. Barker to teach "hard science, not mythology."

Mother, who came across in the article as some kind of liberal superhero, wasn't so sure that the case would have been decided in her favor, as the court might have found that Mrs. Barker's First Amendment rights outweighed the other factors in the case. "Either way," she said, "we all dodged a bullet here: me, the school district, your teacher and especially Judge Harris." She added that "the case would have gone all the way to the Supreme Court," and I wasn't quite sure whether she was relieved or regretted the fact that it hadn't.

With the lawsuit out of the way, I felt confident that things would calm down at school, at least until the lecture series began in a few more weeks. There were no more bricks hurled through our windows, and I was no longer finding Osama Tim Laden posters at school. There were, however, two incidents that gave me pause.

The first such "incident" wasn't much of an incident at all. It was in homeroom, where Mr. Wilson was passing out one of the many forms the school seemed to torture us with each week. Bob Berg handed me the stack of papers and leaned in close to me. He'd been smoking, a vile habit that the borderline criminal crowd had recently taken to, and I felt nauseated as he whispered to me.

"Better watch your back, Jew boy," he said ominously.

The whispered warning hardly impressed me in and of itself, as someone was telling me pretty much on a daily basis that I was going to die one way or another. What struck me was more the choice of the epithet "Jew boy," which you, as an attentive reader, will recall was part of the message on the brick that had landed on the floor of my family's living-room.

To me this seemed to indicate one of two things—apart, of course, from the obvious point that Bad Bob Berg was a bigot and a fool—i.e. that Berg either *was* the person who tossed the brick, or that he had contact with the person or persons responsible. I based my conclusion on the fact that no one else had called me "Jew boy" before or since the stone-throwing incident, and that the association "anti-creationist = Jew" was based on such ignorance that two people could not possibly have come up with it independently of one another. (Or could they?)

The other, rather more serious, incident that helped me to realize that the calm I was experiencing was nothing but a respite before a cataclysmic event happened, of all places, at my church.

I had taken to more regular attendance since the whole evolution v. creationism discussion had burst into my life. I found that going to church was helping me in a variety of ways. For one, attending services regularly made me feel less of a heathen. At school people were openly praying for my salvation, accusing me of being the antichrist or even some sort of terrorist; at church I was one of the fold, just another good little Christian following the Fourth Commandment. (Or the Third, depending on your religion.)

This particular Sunday I didn't feel quite so comfortable in my church; in fact, I had the distinct feeling that people were staring at me. I checked for all the usual suspects—hair mussed, a stain on my shirt, fly open—but found no reasonable explanation for the looks people were casting my way. After a time I realized that they weren't just looking; they actually appeared uncomfortable with my presence. I reasoned that my becoming a social pariah could not in any way be connected with my publicly taken stand on evolution: this was a Unitarian church, after all, and Unitarians by their very nature don't feel particularly strongly about their beliefs, such as they are. Why, then, was I being treated as if I had a communicable disease?

The answer to my query came at the end of the service, as the congregation was filing out past the pastor, whom everyone referred to fondly as Pastor Ron. I didn't make it my habit to shake Pastor Ron's hand or tell him what a terrific sermon he'd given, so I was in the middle of the crowd when I heard him call my name. "Timothy? Timothy, could you stay on for a few minutes?"

I shuffled off to one side and waited for the other parishioners to leave. When we were alone, Pastor Ron closed the doors and said with a forced casualness, "I was rather surprised to see you here today, Timothy."

Our church boasted fairly good attendance, so I supposed the good reverend simply hadn't noticed that I'd stepped up the frequency of my visits. "I've been here just about every Sunday for some time, Pastor Ron," I said as I helped him to collect the hymnals that people had left lying in the pews.

"Oh, I know that, Timothy. I just assumed that you wouldn't be coming any more—you know, since the ..." He seemed to drift off.

"Since the *what*, Pastor Ron?" I was truly puzzled. "Is this about the whole creation v. evolution controversy? Because I can explain."

Now it was Pastor Ron's turn to be puzzled. "Creation v. ...? Controversy? No, I ... I'm talking about the email."

I felt as if I was in some bizarre game of ping pong in which, instead of a ball, we were volleying puzzlement back and forth. "What email are you referring to?"

"There's more than one?"

"Erm, of course," I said, putting a stack of books on the table at the back of the church. "I send emails all the time."

"Somehow, Timothy," Pastor Ron grunted as he put down his stack of books, "I get the impression you don't know what I'm talking about."

The two of us headed for the church office, where the pastor wanted to show me the email on his computer. When we arrived in his cramped office, the computer was already running, and I started when I saw the pastor's screen saver: it was a rather frightening rendition of Satan as half man, half beast, with an extremely prominent erection.

Pastor Ron has never tried to hide the fact that he is gay from the congregation, even having had a commitment ceremony with his partner Don at the church, but still I found these graphic graphics inappropriate.

"That," he said, pointing with obvious distaste toward his computer screen, "is the result of your email."

"I never sent you an email, Pastor Ron," I protested.

"Your name was on it, Timothy," he said.

I moved toward the computer. "May I?"

"Go ahead," he said. "It's fucked anyway."

I tried not to show my shock at a man of the cloth cursing like a common prostitute (not that I know any prostitutes, common or otherwise) and calmly asked why he hadn't simply turned off the computer.

"The virus came with a warning not to. A voice said that any attempt to stop the program from running its course would bring on the fires of hell."

"Running its course?"

"Yes, it said to leave the computer on until Monday. Then it would be over."

"Did it say 'over'?" I almost shouted at the poor man.

"Yes, I think so. Why? Is that important?"

"Maybe," I said pensively. Then I hit a key.

Whoever had programmed this virus had a sense of humor. When I hit the key, Satan's face grew to fill the entire screen and laughed—well, diabolically, and extremely loudly. Using a few hacker's tricks, I was finally able to access the registry, where I found the culprit and isolated it. A quick glance at the directory showed that there was probably no permanent damage, but if my suspicions were correct, this Satanic virus was a variant of the "Game over" virus and would have, at the appointed hour, deleted everything on the pastor's hard drive.

"OK, Pastor Ron, I've disconnected your computer from the network and isolated the virus. Nothing more should happen. But you really need to install anti-virus software."

"I've been meaning to do that," the visibly shaken reverend said. "I guess I always figured nobody would target a church."

"Can you call up your email program for me, please?" I asked. "I'd like to see this email that I supposedly sent."

And there it was. For all intents and purposes, the email appeared to have been sent from my account. I'd have to find out later whether my account had been hacked, or whether somebody had tweaked the email so that it showed my address as the sender. (This is easier than it sounds, unfortunately…) I forwarded myself a copy so that I could ponder that problem later.

The scary part came when I looked at the text of the email. "I am Timothy Thompson, and I am the antichrist," it began, and it went rather downhill from there. The ramblings stated that Christ had never walked the earth in human form, and that I had been sent by the Evil One to do his bidding.

Looking up from the screen I said to Pastor Ron, "Most of this doesn't make a lot of sense."

"It looks like a cut-and-paste job from different parts of the Bible," Pastor Ron explained. "John mostly." Then, after a pause, "I take it you didn't write it?"

"No. But tell me, did other people get this same email? Because I noticed people giving me the evil eye during the service."

"About fifteen parishioners said their computers were infected. What's going to happen?"

"Well, it depends. It looks to me like the 'Game over' virus," I told him. "The more benign versions erase certain kinds of files only—photos, say. Worst case scenario is that it deletes everything on the hard disc."

"Oh my God," the pastor said. "All our records!"

"How many computers are on the church network?"

"With this one, six," he answered. "Why, do you think they're infected, too?"

"Probably," I said. "But I should be able to manage five more. Can you start them up for me?"

Pastor Ron looked embarrassed. "One of them, yes. But the others are password-protected. Only the people who use them can boot them." He emphasized the word "boot" to show that he wasn't a complete technical dummy.

"Can you call them and ask them to come in? It's important we delete the virus before midnight. We also need to call everyone whose computer is affected and fix their computers. I have two friends who can help."

"OK, let's get to work!"

"Oh, Pastor Ron? Could you please tell everybody I had nothing to do with the email or the virus?"

With help from Josh and Stuart—and the pastor's partner Don, who drove them from service call to service call—we were able to repair all the affected computers but two: one at the church because Sally Bradshaw, one of the volunteers, was on vacation, and one at the home of a parishioner for whom the church oddly had no address or phone number.

"Not bad for a day's work," Don said as the five of us sat at my favorite pizzeria wolfing down hard-earned slices that Pastor Ron had sprung for. "But what's the story? I mean, why did somebody want this whole thing pinned on you, Timothy?"

So I told him.

Chapter 23
Projects Update

Meanwhile, I was valiantly balancing my school work (admittedly negligible in quantity and challenge) and various projects. First and foremost was, of course, the lecture series.

It had now been agreed that the lectures were to take place on four consecutive days at the beginning of December, which really seemed to rile the fundamentalists: they were certain that our presentation of evolution was all part of a Jewish-Muslim-communist-atheist plot to wage war on Christmas. In actual fact the dates were chosen according to more prosaic considerations: auditorium schedules (after the annual school play and before the year-end concerts, but not on a pep-rally Friday), guest speaker Cyrus Abrams' availability, Mr. Grass's father's retirement party and, for reasons that eluded me, an apparently long-planned baby shower for the vice principal's secretary.

Josh and I were spending an hour or so after school almost every day preparing for our shock-and-awe presentation. We were stretching

Power Point™ as well as animation programs to the limit to produce a slide show that would have evolution doubters flocking over to our side. Our contribution had to be good, as we were in charge of Day 2, following Cyrus Abrams' keynote opener on Day 1. The expression "a hard act to follow" comes to mind whenever I think of having to speak in this slot, as the good professor is noted for his oratorical skills.

Working with Josh was uncomplicated, in the way that good friends and aging couples seem to have with one another. Each seemed to anticipate the other's thoughts, and even our tastes in graphic design overlapped uncannily. The only things that bothered me were his constant insistence that his parents were going to kill, maim or at the very least disown him, as he was going to hell for what we were doing, and the fact that he was, for lack of a better word, clingy.

At the beginning of our cooperation I had suggested—ever so gently—that we could perhaps work with Megan, especially since Josh intended to remain behind the scenes for our presentation. My best friend, however, found all manner of flimsy excuses why working with *her*—he seemed to be avoiding saying Megan's name—was not to our advantage. I subsequently dropped the issue; after all, I still had biology class, where Megan was my lab partner, and I had finally recognized that having Josh around while I was trying to court Megan would only prove a hindrance.

In addition to our Science Club project, Project Mikey was taking up a great deal of my time. Not that I minded—on the contrary. I enjoyed our sessions, even after the Midwestern winter had arrived, late but with a vengeance, although it meant that my basketball lessons had to be put on hold.

I mentioned earlier the problem of Mike's learning best while in motion, and I was concerned that the winter months would prove an insurmountable problem. In the end I was able to solve the problem with the help of—of all people—Coach Braun.

The coach had let up on me somewhat since learning that I was helping his star player pass ninth grade. Still, when he wasn't thinking, which was distressingly often, his anti-nerd instincts kicked in and caused him to torture me, but the abuse decreased in two dimensions at least: intensity and duration.

It was after a particularly tortuous gym class that I approached Mr. Braun. "Coach?" I said from just outside his office, still in my gym gear. He looked up expectantly, then, upon realizing who it was disturbing his post-sadistic reverie, cast me a disdainful, "Yeah, whaddaya want?"

"Well, sir," I began, maintaining still that politeness can calm even the most agitated of beasts, "I was hoping you had a minute to talk about something."

I could tell from the pained expression on his face that he was thinking. On the one hand, he wanted desperately to turn me away; on the other hand, he was curious what the pathetic little geek wanted from him. And then there was the Mother factor to consider: had he done anything that might lead to litigation that he could fend off with a conversation? Whether it was this fear or the curiosity that got the better of him, he graciously offered, "OK, but just one minute." He looked at his watch demonstratively.

"Thank you," I said, then began the spiel I had rehearsed in front of the mirror that morning. I had timed it and knew I could not possibly finish in the requisite 60 seconds, so I spoke as quickly as possible and hoped that he would find me so engaging that he would hear me out till the end.

"Well, Coach, thing is, I'm friends with Mike Petersson, and I've been tutoring him for a while now."

"Yeah, I heard."

"It seems to be helping, as his grades are up in just about every subject."

Coach Braun snorted at this, which admittedly reeked of self-praise, but I continued. "At first it seemed that Mike wasn't able to retain anything, but then I ascertained that he's a kinesthetic learner."

The coach winced at my last sentence, which contained at least three words that he probably found challenging, something I hadn't taken into account while rehearsing our talk. "He's a what?"

"A kinesthetic learner," I repeated, "although he apparently belongs more to a subset of kinesthetic learners: he needs to be moving in order to absorb new information."

I paused briefly while that last bit of information sank in. Coach Braun confirmed its having done so with a loud harrumph, so I went on.

"I do most of the tutoring on his driveway basketball court, playing one-on-one." I ignored the look of disbelief and continued without interruption. "But it's getting kind of cold for that."

I saw that Mr. Braun was nodding, almost imperceptibly, as I spoke. He was obviously following me better than I had expected, so I refrained from finishing my speech and cut straight to the chase, as they say. "So anyway, I was wondering if the school could help us out?"

"A treadmill," the coach said, somewhat elliptically.

"Exactly," I said, "or maybe a stationary bike."

"I'll see what I can do and get back to you," he said in an almost friendly tone. Then he snarled, "Now hurry up and get your street clothes on. I ain't gonna write you no note when you're late for your next class."

Mr. Braun came through for Mike and me, though he never did "get back" to me. Instead I found that a very expensive and brand-new Nordic Track™ device had been delivered to the Petersson home that very afternoon. Batshit Bob's Sporting Goods had sent it over "on permanent loan" as part of their sponsoring deal with the school's athletic department. Bob had even included a complimentary bat.

Mike was on it when I arrived that evening. "Just look at this thing, Timmy!" he beamed.

"That's great, Mikey," I said. "But I hope you haven't been on it for too long. We've got an hour and a half of studying to do."

"No prob," he said, jumping off the machine while it was moving at full throttle. "Here, I gotta show you something."

Mike opened his backpack and began scrounging about in it. After a few moments he produced a piece of paper and thrust it before my eyes.

As my eyes focused on the page, I saw that it was a math test he'd got back from the teacher. C+!

I, of course, would have been devastated to get this grade on a test in any subject, but I knew that for Mike this was quite an achievement. "That's fantastic!" I shouted and high-fived him. He ignored my outstretched arm and instead picked me up in a bear hug and twirled me around while jumping up and down. I was grateful for the cathedral ceiling.

Just then Mrs. Petersson came into the room and said, laughing, "You boys are in a good mood! What's going on?"

At that point I hoped Mike would release me, as he was pressing a little too hard on my ribcage, but he merely transferred his grip to under my armpits and held me up like a doll he'd brought for show-and-tell. "Timmy here," he said, bobbing me dangerously close to the ceiling, "is a genius. I just got my math test back, Mom. I got a C+!"

Mrs. Petersson's bemused smile turned into a look of unmitigated joy. She ran to give her son a hug, which prompted him to put me down. It felt good to feel the earth beneath my feet again, and I stepped back to admire the scene of genuine mother-son affection as Mrs. Petersson wrapped her arms as far as they would go around her burly boy. Then it was my turn. I found her spontaneous display of affection at once touching and embarrassing. Touching, for it was nothing like anything I'd ever experienced with my own mother, and embarrassing because feeling the warmth of her breasts against me was making me both uncomfortable and strangely agitated.

After releasing me from her embrace, Mrs. Petersson said, "This calls for a celebration, you two. Can you stay for supper, Timothy?"

I left a message at home, knowing that no one would hear it until I myself erased it later that evening, and gratefully accepted the invitation. Mike and I got in a full two hours of studying before dinner. He was even more motivated than usual, and fast-walking on his new treadmill for 120 minutes in addition to the 35 he told me he'd done before my arrival didn't seem to phase him. In fact it was me who was getting tired in the end. Mike said it was from lack of physical activity and offered to bring his weights to the den so that I could work out while tutoring him from then on. I knew I was really going to miss basketball until spring.

Supper was a creamy tuna fish casserole that Mrs. Petersson made from scratch, apparently one of her specialties. She apologized profusely that it wasn't something "a little fancier" almost as often as I told her how delicious it was. And it was! It took me a while to convince her that I wasn't just being polite when I asked her to send my dad the recipe, and she agreed to do so by email as soon as we finished. I also got her recipe for a sweet and sour salad dressing, which was very special. For dessert she served an apple pie that was particularly delectable, but when I asked her what was in it, she confessed that it was store-bought.

Even better than the meal itself, however, was the conversation. I suppose that's what families do at meal-time: talk. But I was nonetheless impressed at the easy nature of the discourse, unlike dinners at our house, where the "pulling teeth" cliché seems completely appropriate.

While preparing our Science Club project, trying to keep Josh happy and utterly enjoying Project Mikey, I was neglecting my other freshman year project, which I like to think of as Project Lotus Blossom.

As you will recall, I had vowed to make Megan Chow my girlfriend before the school year drew to a close. Although I had priceless time with her during biology dissections and many a lunch period spent next to or across from her, what was missing in order to implement my plan was some alone time.

Time was an exceedingly rare commodity for me during those first few months of high school, and I was starting to doubt whether I'd be able to set Project Lotus Blossom in motion before Christmas. I had all but resigned myself to this delay when a most extraordinary thing happened: Megan asked me to go out with her!

Admittedly, it wasn't as exciting as all that. It wasn't a "date" she had in mind—at least it didn't start out that way. One day at the end of a biology lab, when Megan and I were returning our instruments to our respective drawers and arranging them the way Mrs. Barker had taught us, she sprang it on me: "Timothy, can we talk?"

"Of course," I said. "We've been talking all along. Erm, haven't we?"

"Well, yes," she stammered, "but I was thinking maybe … outside school."

"OK, sure. I usually meet Josh after school, then I head over to Mike Petersson's to tutor him." I was talking at break-neck speed and feeding her irrelevant information out of nervousness. "But tomorrow Mike is at an away game, so we could meet when I'm done with Josh. 4:15 maybe?"

"OK, fine," my sweet Megan replied. "Then we can head over to The Dairy and have a soda or something."

For all you non-Batshitian readers, The Dairy is a soda-fountain type place near our school, which my parents assure me hasn't changed one iota since they went to school. Being the closest place of business to Batshit High, it is both a traditional after-school hangout and a favorite dating spot. The next 29 hours were sheer torture, as I didn't know whether we were going to hang out or to have a date.

The appointed time for our meeting eventually arrived. Megan was at the school's main entrance just as we'd discussed, and I managed to be on time. I didn't tell Josh about the meeting; it was hard enough to get him to let go of me even without telling him I was going to meet Megan. My feelings for her had become somewhat of a sore spot with my best school friend—understandable considering the number of times I had professed my undying love for her when talking to Josh.

On the walk to The Dairy, Megan was oddly silent. I took my cue from her and said nothing. Ten feet or so from the entrance she spoke.

"Timothy."

"Yes?"

"I don't know how to do this," she said somewhat mysteriously.

"Do what?"

"I don't know if I should ask you or just tell you."

We were stopped in front of the big picture windows of The Dairy. I saw that the place was full of students from our school, mostly older, many with letter jackets or cheerleader uniforms. A few at the tables along the window front were looking at us, not out of interest in us, but more out of the general ennui that seems to be a part of teenage existence. I was keenly aware that this was not the best time to make a scene.

"Ask or tell me what?" I sounded vaguely exasperated, but to the casual observers within, my demeanor was nothing if not cool, calm and collected.

"If you're gay!" The words burst out of Megan, and I hoped there were no lip-readers watching us.

"You were going to ask me if I'm gay?" I tried to compose myself and move my lips as little as possible. "And what were you going to tell me?"

"That's what people are saying, Timothy," my lotus blossom said.

"But why? Why are they saying that?"

"So you don't deny it?"

"No. I mean yes." Ah, Timothy, the epitome of clarity. "Megan, I thought we were coming here on a date."

"You did? Why?"

"Well, it's kind of what guys and girls do—when they like each other, I mean. Did you ask me here to confront me about being gay?"

"So you *are* gay? I'm confused."

"Me too."

"A lot of people our age are confused about their sexuality, Timothy. I've been reading up on it. And it's OK," she assured me. "I just want you to know that if you ever feel the need to talk, I'm here for you."

I opened my mouth in protest, but nothing came out.

"Look, I can see you're not ready, and I understand. Just let me know if and when you *are* ready, and we can meet again. OK?"

She followed her offer with a peck on the cheek, which under most circumstances would have made me swoon. Instead it gave me the courage to speak. "I'm not gay, Megan."

"No?" She looked surprised.

"No."

"Are you sure? Because it's OK if you are."

"Yes, I'm sure. I think I'd know if I were."

"Not necessarily," she began. "From what I read, …"

I interrupted her. "Megan, I'm sure. I'm not gay."

"Oh."

"You sound disappointed," I pointed out.

"I had this whole speech prepared," she explained. "I wanted to show how accepting I can be."

"So why did you want to come here?" I motioned toward the inside of The Dairy.

"I thought we could take care of the whole gay thing on the way here. And then we could go in and look like we were together, so people would stop saying you're gay. I thought I could be your beard."

"My beard?"

"That's what they call women who cover for gay guys." And when I looked at her quizzically, she added, "I told you I've been reading up on this."

"Well, I don't need a 'beard'," I told her, "but it's really nice of you. I'd have liked looking like we're together."

"We still can," she smiled.

So we went inside and not only looked like we were together. Project Lotus Blossom was finished successfully even before I'd officially begun work on it. And I really didn't care why anybody thought I was gay.

Chapter 24
Another Rebel With A Cause

Time seemed to fly after Megan's and my first "date" at The Dairy. I still didn't have a lot of time to spend with her, but we managed to meet outside school about once a week. And, although nothing discernible had changed between us, we both knew that our dissections and shared lunches were now extra-special.

I was worried that Josh would be upset about me and Megan, but he didn't seem to notice anything. He was, after all, only jealous of the time I would spend with a girlfriend, and I was still with him most days after school. The true test of our friendship would come when the lecture series was finished and he and I no longer needed to spend so much time together and I could see more of my sweet Megan. And that time was rapidly drawing closer.

Two weeks before the start of the lecture series, the unpleasantness started to pick up again. Our lunch table—or, as we discovered some students had taken to calling it, the "planet of the apes"—began receiving more uninvited and unwanted visits. The two apostles who had once before come to tell us that Jesus loved us now came every day. The ritual was always the same: they stood at one end of the table until we grew silent and looked up toward them, at which point they announced that they were praying for us and that God would forgive us. The girl would put her hand lightly on my shoulder for a second, then withdraw it before the pair looked pityingly on us and slowly left.

I found their behavior a bit creepy, and while we laughed about it the first few times, we later simply took it in stride, barely interrupting our conversation for the absolution and performance.

Somewhat harder to ignore were the jocks who passed our table making chimpanzee noises. The first time it happened, Lamont thought it was some sort of racial taunt, but Clem calmed him down by explaining that these simpletons had reduced the complexities of evolutionary theory to one tiny factoid, the relationship of humans and apes. The zoo sounds became a regular feature of our lunches, occurring as often as four times during the period. One day two boys stopped at the table and pretended to groom each other, searching each other's bodies for invisible lice, which they removed with their fingertips and placed in their mouths. It was an incredibly realistic performance, for which I made an effort to compliment them profusely. It was only when I said that I had really believed I had two apes in front of me that they realized I was being disingenuous and threatened to end my life later that day. Needless to say, they failed to carry out their threat.

Most disturbing for their persistence, however, were the reporters who called us on the phone or bushwhacked us leaving school. Apparently someone had sent our contact info and photos to members of the press, and these people were highly interested in finding out more of what to expect from our lecture series. Fortunately I had warned the others after the reporter had contacted Mother, so they were prepared and knew to say nothing.

Principal Powers, too, was being pestered by persistent press people, and he asked me to his office to talk about it. He again chose gym class as the best time to call me away from lessons, much to Coach Braun's chagrin and my delight.

"Good to see you again, Timothy," Mr. Powers said after Mrs. McDermitt ushered me in.

"Thank you, Mr. Powers. It's good to see you, too."

"Let me get straight to the point, Timothy. I have been receiving inquiries from distinguished members of our nation's fourth estate."

Obviously my poker face needs work, as Mr. Powers immediately recognized that I had no idea what he was talking about. "The fourth estate," he said, "refers to the press. Do look it up, Timothy: the history of the term is fascinating."

"I will, Mr. Powers, thank you." (I did look it up, by the way, and found it to be interesting, though not fascinating.) I continued, "So you've been contacted by reporters? Concerning the evolution lectures?"

"That is correct. Word has got out, and there promises to be considerable coverage, and not just locally either. The school board is getting nervous."

"Sir, just so you know: I didn't breathe a word of this to anybody. And all of us in the Science Club are avoiding talking to reporters."

"I know you didn't contact the press corps, Timothy. I did."

"*You* did? Erm, may I ask why?"

The principal let out a lengthy sigh as he sat back and gazed at his hands, whose fingers were touching like a spider on a mirror. When he closed his eyes I thought he might have dozed off. But then, after a few moments, he spoke.

"Remember, Timothy, how I said that the school board was getting nervous?"

"Yes?"

"Well, that's why. That's my reason."

I thought I detected a mischievous grin on the old man's face as he said this. Suddenly he opened his eyes and leapt forward out of his chair. As he paced, he held a monologue, a shortened version of which I transcribe below.

"I have been an educator for a very long time, and I have seen many an educational reform come and go. When I first got my degree, rote learning was considered essential to the development of the young mind. That quickly went out of fashion, and we embraced various trends, both in individual subjects and in pedagogy in general. The reforms went by all kinds of fancy names: Phonics, New Math, Audio-Lingual Learning, Computer-Aided Learning, Bilingual Education, No Child Left Behind, Multi-Culturalism.

"Most of us went about implementing each and every one of these supposedly new approaches with enthusiasm. I know I did. That's how I got to be principal, back somewhere between the Ark and the Roman Empire.

"There was one thing I learned from all this 'progress': students—at least the good ones—will learn no matter what we do. We can facilitate their quest for knowledge, or we can make it difficult, but no matter what we in the business of shaping young minds do, children and teen-agers will learn. That's the beauty of it.

"Among all these reforms there has of late been a rather disturbing tendency in our schools and our society in general. For lack of a better description, I like to call it the crusade of ignorance. Nefarious forces are loose, and whatever their professed purpose may be, their effect is the same: to usurp our educational system and to fill young minds with so much hooey.

"Let me tell you, young man," he said, addressing me directly for the first time, "this frightens the hell out of me."

Mr. Powers stood behind his massive leather armchair, his hands squeezing the firm upholstery. "I wouldn't want you to think me an alarmist, Timothy, but I'm scared to death of the path down which our country and our schools are headed. It's why I haven't retired yet."

I pondered what my principal had just told me as a heavy silence fell over the room. After a minute, I finally dared to speak.

"These 'forces' you're talking about, Mr. Powers," I ventured, "are you talking about fundamentalist Christians?"

Mr. Powers smiled benevolently, as one does to a small child who has said something charming about a subject he knows nothing about.

"I'm talking about fundamentalists of all kinds. Let me explain. Once upon a time, there was a virtue known as tolerance. We all preached it and some of us tried to live by it.

"Fundamentalists of a certain ilk perverted that concept by taking it to extremes. Suddenly we were to tolerate everything, the lines between right and wrong became blurred. Out of that was born 'political correctness.'

"It was no longer 'PC' to say someone else's ideas or especially their beliefs were wrong. Facts became less relevant to discussion, and we began to show open disdain towards experts because they were seen as the keepers of the facts, and facts only got in the way of what we believed. Informed debate went out of fashion.

"Eventually we got where we are today. Have you ever tried having a discussion about global warming? If you have, I suspect you cited facts, referenced experts. That's the way we used to have discussions, debates. The person with logic, with facts, with experts on his side won the argument.

"Nowadays there's always somebody in the room who has his beliefs, the facts be damned. And those of us who have the studies, the research on our side are expected to tolerate their ignorance of the facts. Well, I won't have it any more!"

So my principal was a rebel! And an impassioned one at that. I was still not clear on a few things, however.

"Would I be correct in assuming that there are fundamentalists on the school board, and that they're the ones getting nervous?"

"Yes, that would be a fair assessment," Mr. Powers replied. "But not fundamentalist Christians who doubt evolution, if that's what you mean; instead we have fundamentalists in tolerance who are uncomfortable taking on the forces of ignorance."

"My mother doesn't want me to use the word *ignorant* when I talk about Christian fundamentalists. Do you think she's being too tolerant?"

"Timothy, I've met your mother. I found her a most impressive individual, but I would disagree with her on this particular point. I am a great believer in calling a spade a spade. The word *ignorant* comes from the verb *to ignore*, and people who *choose* to ignore facts because they prefer to believe in something else are ignorant in the truest sense of the word.

"As an educator I see it as my duty to fight this most reprehensible brand of ignorance because it will inevitably lead to another kind of ignorance: ignorance born not out of choice, but because facts were deliberately withheld."

"So I take it the press will be at our lectures?"

"Yes, they will. And as many members of the general public as our auditorium can accommodate. That's actually why I called you in, Timothy, to tell you that. I hadn't planned to give you a lecture."

"I'm very glad you did, sir," I said. "It's given me a lot to think about. If I may say so, I'm happy that you feel so strongly about evolution."

"Actually, I don't," Mr. Powers contradicted. "I'm a Greek scholar— a bit of an expert in fact. When I tell people outside my field of expertise that every serious scholar in my field interprets a particular text in a certain way, I don't expect them to contradict me. I expect them to accept what I say as fact.

"And as I think I've made amply clear, I'm a great believer in facts. As far as evolution is concerned, experts in the relevant fields of biology and paleontology tell me that evolution is a fact. Who am I to doubt them? Which is not to say I don't wish to learn more. I will be sitting in the front row of the auditorium when Professor Abrams, you and the others enlighten us with your knowledge of the facts."

Almost by way of punctuation, the bell rang for third period at the end of Mr. Powers' last sentence.

"Now go, Timothy. It's time for your biology lesson."

As I headed out the door, Mr. Powers called to me. "And Timothy? I'd appreciate it if what I said about the school board remained between the two of us."

"Of course," I agreed. "Oh, Mr. Powers, one other thing: I think Mrs. Barker may be planning to take a field trip to a creationist museum. I don't think …"

"Not to worry, Timothy," the old man said. "That has already been dealt with."

Impressive, I thought. The man obviously has his sources. But, I suspected, he was not the only one. I only hoped for Mike's sake that the field trip would still go ahead, though to a legitimate destination. (It did.)

As I left the principal's office, I noticed that Mrs. McDermitt was wearing earphones, ostensibly to type something up from dictation. At the same time I couldn't help but notice that the screen saver on her computer monitor was on, a sure sign that she hadn't been working. I wished her a pleasant day and left her office for the chaos of the halls.

Chapter 25

The Final Stretch

The meeting with Principal Powers at which he gave me his "crusade of ignorance" speech was a sort of starting pistol for the final stretch leading up to the evolution lectures. After that, more and more people seemed to be getting into the act.

Mr. Wilson, my homeroom teacher, was the first member of faculty I noticed demonstrating support for our cause, although I am sure very few people were observant enough to catch the tiny button this hulk of a man sported on his shirt collar, and fewer still would recognize the black-and-white portrait of a balding, bearded gentleman as Charles Darwin. Nonetheless I was touched by the gesture. At first I thought he might get in trouble for advertising his political leanings in school, but then I remembered that Darwinism was about science, not politics. It was the other side that would have us believe otherwise.

Mr. Leitner, as a social studies teacher, was able to take on the topic more directly. He decided—on what for all intents and purposes appeared to be the spur of the moment—to delay further discussion of the issues involved in the United States Civil War and jump ahead a few decades to the 1925 Scopes Trial in Dayton, Tennessee.

For those unfamiliar with the Scopes case, it involved a young biology teacher who deliberately violated a Tennessee statute which prohibited the teaching of evolution. Two of America's finest orators tried the case. William Jennings Bryan, a popular Democratic politician, argued for the prosecution, while Clarence Darrow, according to Mother the most brilliant trial lawyer ever to have lived, took up the biology teacher's defense. Reason and science formally lost the trial, but most observers agreed that Darrow had made a fool of Bryan by calling him as an expert witness on the Bible after all his expert witnesses on matters of science had been rejected.

Ms. Pewney, in addition to coaching us in presentation techniques, brought out some dusty old tomes with a play based on the Scopes Trial, and we read *Inherit the Wind*. The authors renamed everyone in the story for reasons I cannot fathom, and they even added a disclaimer stating that the play is not based on any actual event, although it clearly is. Be that as it may, they have their Bryan character, while being quizzed on matters of geology, making the particularly revealing statement that he is "more interested in the Rock of Ages than the age of rocks."

> *[Aside: People who believe in the creation myth often believe that the earth is less than 10,000 years old, with 6,000 being the most often mentioned number, although many rocks—and for that matter Chinese civilization—are demonstrably older. "Rock of Ages" is a Christian hymn.]*

Even Ms. O'Toole, my math teacher, joined in the fun and games, although I doubt whether anyone else noticed. When I got to her room one afternoon, I saw that she'd written the following on the board: 4.54×10^9. That happens to be the best estimate of the age of the earth, 4.54 billion years.

Yes, I am aware that the fact that I immediately recognized the meaning of this number makes me a major geek, but I find it somewhat disconcerting that not one single student from any grade or level of achievement asked Ms. O. what the numbers that featured so prominently on her board meant. (She told me this.) The numbers stayed up on the whiteboard for two entire weeks, and the dowdy Ms. O'Toole went out of her way to call attention to them by demonstratively erasing around them, yet not one student so much as asked what the numbers signified. This lack of intellectual or even casual curiosity astounds me and will, I am convinced, be the bane and lead to the eventual ruin of Western civilization, possibly within my lifetime.

Miss Abrams did an exceedingly creative display in the library, decking the whole room out in a nautical theme to commemorate the fact that Darwin wrote *On the Origin of Species* after his legendary journey aboard a sloop called HMS *Beagle*. Interspersed among the paraphernalia were photos of birds Darwin had seen on the Galapagos Islands. It was the distribution of the bird species and various fossils that led him to draw conclusions about common origins of species and natural selection.

She had also installed glass cases at strategic spots around the library, in which she displayed some rather remarkable fossils her father must have given her. In one case there was even what looked to be a first-edition copy of Darwin's seminal work, along with modern discussions of Darwinian theory. She told me that she'd originally hung a banner that read "Read your Darwin," but that Mr. Powers had quietly suggested that people more familiar with the admonition to "Read your Bible" might be offended. Despite the fact that that had been precisely her intent, she thought it best to take the banner down. The display remained untitled.

I also received reports from sympathizers about other teachers who were making their opinions known prior to our lecture series. Apparently one of the art teachers painted or commissioned his very own Sistine Chapel. A huge replica of Michelangelo's famous ceiling centerpiece, in which the hand of God touches Adam's hand, thus bringing him and all of humanity to life, had appeared on an art room ceiling over the weekend. Unfortunately I was unable to independently verify that, and my only comment would be that the Sistine Chapel may be great art, but it's not science.

Our school forbids students and staff from professing their political beliefs in school, and of course religious expression is not allowed either, so people got creative. Naturally anyone was free to show support for science, so some T-shirts with Darwin, Einstein sticking out his tongue or with $E = mc^2$ appeared. A few students even showed up with motifs that showed the chain of species leading up to the modern horse or, heaven forbid, humans. All these were, of course, isolated, as most students found that they couldn't care less about the issue.

The creationists had a rather more difficult time making their opinions known. The well-known fish symbol of Christianity was obviously off limits, but a T-shirt depicting a real fish was not. Also, I'm sure the makers of the *Finding Nemo* film—or "flick," as Megan would have it—were surprised at the revival in Nemo merchandise in our area of the Midwest: lots of Nemo key chains were hung from backpacks, and a few Nemo lunch boxes were spotted in the cafeteria. (Josh was thrilled to see the lunch boxes—vintage, no less—and even managed to convince himself that he had started a trend, however small.) My German teacher took to drinking out of a Nemo mug. It made me wonder how Christ would have felt about his religion being represented by a clownfish with a crippled fin. The two apostles who came to our lunch table every day started wearing "I ❤ Nemo" T-shirts—all perfectly legal, all perfectly clear in their message.

Less clear were the BFJ buttons that cropped up. My lunch group racked its brains for several days before Clem finally approached a girl wearing one and asked what it meant. We were, frankly, stunned by the answer: "Batshit for Jesus."

The one person who was most conspicuous by her absence from the fray was the woman who had started it all: Mrs. Barker. Until the Friday before the lecture series began, she didn't say a word about it. I didn't detect any kind of subtle display—Nemo or otherwise. All she said on the subject came at the end of the period on Friday.

"Don't forget that our class will convene in the auditorium on Monday, at the usual time. And yes: attendance is mandatory."

That was all. She didn't look askance at me, say anything derogatory about the purpose of the convocation in the auditorium, or attempt to nail me to a cross. In fact, I have to say that Mrs. Barker's behavior toward me and in regard to the evolution lectures had been, for lack of a better word, Christian.

The lectures were, as the expression goes, the "elephant in the room": everyone knows it's there, but no one dares talk about it. Except for the brief discussion I had had with Mrs. Barker just after the lecture series was decided and this mention in class, she had ignored it altogether. I assumed that she would, however, have questions ready for Cyrus Abrams, questions that would look as if she was trying to obtain clarification of a point of fact but which actually would serve as propaganda for her unscientific creationist beliefs. The thought angered me at first, but when I mulled over it I arrived at the conclusion that I would do no differently were I in her situation. I decided that I was looking forward to seeing how the famous professor dealt with a dyed-in-the-wool fundamentalist.

Chapter 26

Visitors

To say that the final weekend before the beginning of our lecture series on evolution was eventful would be tantamount to severely understating the facts.

Josh and I didn't want to over-prepare our presentation, so we had decided against meeting after school on that last Friday. Truth be told, our presentation had been finished for more than a week, and we had been meeting more out of habit than necessity over the final week. Josh hadn't changed his mind about staying in the background, so I was going to be alone on stage, which I wasn't particularly pleased about. So our practice sessions were really about me getting used to speaking while operating our rather elaborate Power Point presentation and Josh timing me with a stopwatch and taking notes about where our slides still needed tweaking.

Mike had an away game that evening, so I didn't have to tutor him either. (Yes, we normally met on Fridays too.) That meant that I was free to see Megan! Unfortunately, by the time I asked her whether she was available, she had already made plans to go to the mall with some of her female friends. She generously asked me to join them, but, although everyone at school still seemed to think I'm gay, I really don't enjoy shopping. (If it is a homophobic stereotype that gay men like to shop, I apologize. From my limited observation and what I have heard on television, however, I do believe it to be true.)

I went home that Friday evening expecting to have a quiet time of it, perhaps nuking some mac and cheese and playing video games. Before I turned the corner of our street I could already smell the pungent cheese, and I was looking forward to my online game group, who had probably given me up for dead, as much as I had neglected them these past weeks.

When I arrived on our street, I was surprised to see people milling about. It was a smallish group—nine by my quick count—and they were congregating in front of the house four up from ours. I walked past them and thought I heard one of them whisper, "That's him." I chose to ignore it and went home.

Inside I heard once again the unmistakable sounds of Goth Girl and her mysterious visitor: Satanic chants, conversation and laughter emanating from upstairs. Since I had nothing to do, I thought that tonight would be the night I would finally catch a glimpse of the visitor. Although I deemed it less than important who it was visiting my otherwise anti-social sibling, I could not deny my considerable curiosity as to the identity of the caller: male? female? human? And so I planted myself on an armchair with a view of the stairs and fired up my game console.

As expected, when I logged in to my account, the guys (and one girl) I usually play with were there immediately. "Where you been, dude?" was the general tenor of their greetings. Such is my understanding of the human condition, however, that I surmised that they didn't expect an answer to their query, so I simply said, "Hey, guys, it's good to be back." As expected, no one missed any kind of explanation for my absence, but simply commenced play as if I'd never been gone. I had really missed the warm embrace of my peers all this time.

We were close to liberating a group of hostages from the hands of terrorists when I detected motion from the direction of the stairway. I briefly redirected my attention from the screen to the black-clad figures moving downward towards me; at that moment I heard the rebuke of a team-mate: "Whaddaya doin', Tim-Tom? You just got me killed, jerkface!"

"Sorry," I mumbled into my mic and logged out.

The black-clad figures, who were now on terra firma with me, were, of course, my sister and her visitor, who proved to be a freakishly tall, lanky, pale but good-looking boy of 16 or 17, making him about my sister's age. Although he was, at his widest, about as thick as one of Goth Girl's legs, and folded over twice could have fit into her torso with room to spare, the two of them looked really good together. I suspect the contrast was part of the effect, but the two of them just looked so completely comfortable with one another that they projected an aura of tranquility.

GG was not wearing her look of studied indifference, but appeared quite—dare I say it?—happy. She didn't exactly have a smile on her face, but her expression and bearing betrayed an inner peace that was most becoming, and which I hadn't seen on her since her thirteenth birthday. I liked her new friend already for the effect he was having on my big sister.

As the two of them approached, the boy cracked a small, crooked smile. "So you're the boy genius I've heard so much about."

That left me flabbergasted beyond words, and on so many levels. For one thing, it sounded, frankly, too adult. Indeed, it was the sort of thing my dad's "buddies" said when we first met, sort of in the same category with "chip off the old block" and "sow your wild oats." Totally incongruous coming from this young Goth. The deeper implication of the statement was that GG had been talking to her friend—boyfriend?—about me, which was most certainly unexpected, given that she hadn't shown any interest in me since the time she got in trouble for dressing me up in Mother's old clothes when I was four.

The main problem I had with a greeting such as "So you're the boy genius I've heard so much about" is that I genuinely do not know how to respond. To confirm it ("Yes, that's me.") sounds more than a little conceited, and to deny it ("Me? No!") rings of false modesty. Dismissing the claim to genius ("Aw, shucks.") is disingenuous at best, transparent in its avoidance and deviousness at worst. So I chose my usual response.

"Hi, I'm Timothy," I said, to which the *Twilight* casting finalist responded, "Hey. I'm Zac."

The ice thus broken, we slipped into casual conversational mode.

"So how's it goin', Timothy?" he asked.

"Good. You?"

"Good. You play Counterstrike™, huh?"

"Yeah. You know it?"

"Yeah, I used to play. Lost interest."

"Oh, right." Was he being dismissive of my pastime?

After an awkward silence, Zac finally broached the subject that had brought the pair of them downstairs in the first place. "Look, Timothy…, Mands and I were wondering if I could come to your dinner on Sunday with Cyrus Abrams?"

Mands? "You'd really have to ask my dad," I said. "And my mother," I added as an afterthought.

"Oh, I will," he interjected. "I just wanted to make sure it was OK with you first. I mean, Professor Abrams is *your* guest."

This new friend of GG's—sorry, of Mands's—was certainly well-mannered. Although it was true that I had been the one to ask Cyrus and Emily Abrams to dinner, I hardly thought of it as *my* invitation, yet Zac wanted to be sure he wasn't infringing. Most considerate. I was still mulling this over in my mind when Zac spoke again, apparently taking my silence as a sign of impending refusal.

"The thing is, I'm kind of a big admirer of Cyrus Abrams. I've read all his books, and I'm thinking of going into biology—maybe even at Northwestern. I thought maybe if I could talk to him, …"

Zac's voice faded out as he continued to misread my lack of an answer. In actual fact, I was so much in awe of his ambition and goals, which were so unexpected, that I was having problems getting my larynx to express my approval.

"Sure," I finally said, "no problem."

"Hey, that's great, thanks, I really appreciate this," Zac said, and I was genuinely afraid he was going to hug me.

Zac and I continued with some inane small talk for a few minutes, until GG/Mands signaled she wanted to withdraw. Zac adeptly drew things to a close.

"Well, it's been good talking to you, Timothy. … Erm, maybe we can play some Counterstrike sometime?"

"I thought you said you lost interest?" I said, perhaps a tad too aggressively.

"Yeah, that was when my dad lost his job and we had to get rid of our broadband. I really only like it when I'm playing with a team."

"OK, let's do that sometime."

And the two headed back upstairs to GG's room. Just as they reached the top of the stairs, the front door opened and Dad walked in.

Instead of the usual, "Hi, everybody, I'm home," Dad said, gesturing toward the outside, "What's with all the people out there?"

I walked to the front room window and pulled back the curtain. As Dad had suggested, a sizable crowd had gathered in front of our house. They seemed to have no particular reason for being there; they simply stood there in small groups talking, many of them hopping from foot to foot, trying to keep warm in the early December air.

I recognized some of the well-bundled people from the much smaller crowd I'd seen outside our neighbor's house before. One of them spotted me behind the curtain and pointed, the others looked curiously in my direction. There was nothing aggressive about the crowd, but they made me nervous nonetheless.

Zac and GG/Mands came back down the stairs and watched with me as four more people arrived on foot and three hopped out of a car.

"There must be like a hundred people out there," said Zac. (The actual figure was 41. Zac apparently liked to exaggerate.)

"Weird," said GG, quite audibly.

I let go of the curtain, for the real show now seemed to be indoors. It took Dad a moment to realize what had happened, but then he tried to shake the cobwebs out of his head and stared disbelievingly in GG's direction. She took no notice, and neither did Zac. I waved my arms to Dad to let him know that he should leave what had just happened uncommented, and eventually he caught on.

I quickly jumped in before things could get awkward.

"Dad, you haven't met Zac," I said, motioning toward our visitor.

Zac snapped out of his momentary stupor and turned to face my father. "Oh, sorry. Mr. Thompson, I'm Zac, Mands's friend." He even extended his hand as he walked toward my dad, whose jaw was still hanging open in astonishment from GG's sudden outburst.

By the time Zac thrust his hand into Dad's, the latter had composed himself and was as gracious as ever. "Nice to meet you, Zac." Then, pointing toward the front of the house, "Those aren't friends of yours, are they?"

"No, sir," the young man answered simply, without knowing he had pressed all the right buttons with my father. My dad likes young people with manners, Gothic garb or not.

"I didn't think so. Anyway, Zac, are you staying for supper? We don't always eat together on Fridays," he said, causing GG to move her head in my direction to catch me with a "WTF" look on my face, "but if you like, you're more than welcome. I'm making lasagna."

"Thanks, Mr. Thompson," this well-mannered youth responded, "that's really nice of you, but my mom is expecting me. I was hoping to join you on Sunday, though, when Professor Abrams is here." Then, sensing some hesitation, he added, "Timothy said it would be all right if it's OK with you and Mrs. Thompson."

I nodded and Dad said, "I'm sure Mrs. Thompson won't object. Be here at 7." Then, looking in my direction he said, "And if you want to invite somebody over, that's OK too."

Outside the crowd had built to a genuine one hundred strong. One very determined-looking, diminutive woman was now corralling them into three lines facing the house, and though they weren't actually doing anything, they looked vaguely threatening.

Zac had his coat on, and before he could open the front door, I suggested he might want to go out the back way and avoid the crowd. I liked him already, and I didn't want to risk anything happening to him when he was obviously so good for my sister.

Zac peeked and agreed, now estimating the crowd at "like five hundred," which was, of course, preposterous, but I have already remarked on his penchant for exaggeration. As he left via the back door, I could hear the crowd outside mangling the classic hymn "Bringing in the Sheaves."

Zac was barely gone and GG was but half-way up the stairs when we heard rattling at the front door. My mind flashed to the chanting mob outside our door, and I immediately assumed the self-defense stance that Mike had taught me. Considering that that was as far as we had gotten with my anti-bullying regimen, it's just as well that it was only Mother fumbling with her keys on her way in.

"What's with the choir of angels out there?" she asked by way of greeting while she took off her gloves. "I couldn't pull into the driveway and had to park half-way down the block. And it's *freezing* out there."

"You poor thing," Dad said in his baby's-got-a-booboo voice. "Let me fix you a nice cup of tea."

"Thanks, Paul," Mother said. "But I think I'd rather have a glass of scotch." She folded herself into her favorite chair.

"Coming right up," Dad offered, disappearing into the kitchen. At he same time I noticed GG sneaking off to her room. I don't think Mother even noticed her.

Mother turned her head toward me. "So what is that outside? Has flash mobbing come to our little stretch of paradise?"

Mother's sense of humor was obviously intact, which meant that this was likely to be a stress-free weekend, for which I was most grateful. I needed to keep my head clear for the coming week: I had drawn the short stick and had to introduce Cyrus Abrams at the assembly on Monday, and on Tuesday I was up for my presentation of Josh's and my work.

"None of us knows what's going on, Mother," I told her. "They just appeared over the last hour." Pulling back the curtain to look again at the assembled masses, I thought I saw, of all people, Mrs. McDermitt. "I suspect it has something to do with the evolution lectures next week."

I fully expected Mother to lash out, either at me or at the crowd of Christians outside, but instead she just said, "You're probably right. A prayer vigil at the home of the heathens was bound to happen."

Dad came in with Mother's drink, and she downed a good chug before thanking him. "Speaking of the lectures, Tracy managed to clear my schedule for Tuesday morning, so I'll be able to come and see you after all."

This was indeed a BIG THING. My mother, I learned from Grandma, had missed my baptism because she had a brief to write. She wasn't at the recital when I learned to play the flute at age five. She begged off on the Thanksgiving Pageant when I had the honor of playing Myles Standish in second grade. And she showed up late for my junior high school graduation, thus missing me getting a gold medal for academic achievement. (She later told me she was just as proud to see the principal present me with a certificate for perfect attendance, which came at the end of the ceremony.) So for her to make an effort to be there for this particular event meant a lot to me.

"Thanks, Mother."

"I wouldn't miss it for the world, Timothy," she said, taking another swig of whisky.

"Ronnie?" Dad said. "What are we going to do about the singers outside?"

"Keep the windows closed, for one thing. The wretched singing was one of the reasons I stopped going to church."

"Yes, but isn't there something you can do to get rid of them?"

"We could pray for a blizzard," Mother suggested. "That might send them on their merry ways."

Dad drew a deep breath. Unlike me, he didn't like it when Mother was in one of her sarcastic moods. "I was thinking more of the legal realm," he said. "An injunction or something?"

"Unfortunately, Paul, even deranged fundamentalists have rights under the First Amendment. Freedom to assemble, freedom of speech—all that."

"But they're on our property," Dad protested.

"Not when I looked," Mother said drily. "They were all standing on the grass between the sidewalk and the street. That's public land, Paul."

"My grass," Dad said. "I'll have to replant with them trampling all over it. Doesn't that count for anything?"

"I suppose we could claim destruction of property," Mother said. "But I won't. I've fought for the First Amendment rights of transsexual students, striking dock workers and neo-Nazis, and I've won every single one of those battles. I can hardly turn around and take these people to court because they're exercising their rights—rights that I have fought for—on a patch of grass that just might need replanting because of it. How would that make me look? Like a damned hypocrite, that's how!"

Dad was frustrated and looking very timid in the face of that onslaught. "You're right," he conceded. "But I don't like it. It's awfully intimidating to have a hundred people singing hymns at you."

"I know. But that's kind of the point of the Bill of Rights, Paul," Mother reminded him. "To protect that which is unpopular."

"Hmph," he replied.

"I do have one idea though," Mother said. "Troops, follow me."

We followed Mother to the kitchen, where she started boiling water, one of the few kitchen skills she has mastered. "Can you two get the big thermoses from the basement and clean them out?" she said to Dad and me. "We're going to smother these fine Christians with kindness."

Half an hour later, Dad, Mother and I were out among the congregation, dispensing hot coffee, cocoa and mulled wine to the faithful. (Interestingly, the mulled wine was the first to run out. A temperate bunch they were not.)

My crafty mother spontaneously started saying "God bless" to each person as she handed them their drink of choice, looking deep into their eyes as she did so. Dad and I followed suit, and soon we were chatting merrily with those who would have intimidated us. The party started to break up at around 10 p.m., with the last of the revelers leaving just after 10:30.

Mrs. McDermitt, who was indeed the person I'd spotted in the crowd earlier, was the last to go. "So much for our all-night vigil," she said with a slight laugh. "Well, see you tomorrow."

"Yes, see you, Molly" Mother said. "And I'll pick up some more of that wine tomorrow morning."

After Mrs. McDermitt pulled away, I looked at my mother. "That was pretty impressive," I said.

"All in a day's work, Timothy," she said. "All in a day's work."

"So being a lawyer isn't all about being ferocious?" I commented.

Mother smiled. "That's a small part of the job. More important is laying on the charm, getting people to do what you want, having them think the whole time that that's what they themselves wanted. Fighting is a last resort. Come on," she said, putting her arm around me for the first time in years. "Let's go inside. Now, could one of you tell me who that was that I saw skulking out the back when I came home? What with all the Christians I saw tonight, I completely forgot about the devil."

Chapter 27

Just Another Saturday
At The Thompsons'

The prayer vigil got off to a slow start on Saturday morning, with the first stragglers showing up at around 11 a.m. I suppose even fanatic supporters of the unsupportable like to sleep in now and then.

My parents seemed to be sleeping in as well, or so I assumed when they didn't show their faces all morning. By 11:30, however, I felt concerned and knocked on their bedroom door. When there was no reaction even after several knocks, I ventured inside. There was no sign of them, and the bedroom looked as if they'd left in a hurry. It was highly unusual for my dad to leave the house without making the bed.

I checked everywhere, even knocking on GG's door. I knew she wouldn't be pleased to be disturbed the wrong side of noon, but nothing could have prepared me for the sight of GG's face when she opened her door.

She'd been crying, and her face was actually flushed. When she saw me, she burst into tears again. Only recently I had heard her voice for the first time in months, now I was witnessing a genuine display of emotion and holding her in my arms, trying to comfort her. The casual observer could be forgiven for assuming we were two normal siblings expressing themselves normally in a moment of distress.

It took me a long time to ascertain just what the cause of all this distress was, and I was assuming the worst. Finally, GG blubbered, "It's Grandma."

I waited a few seconds in the hopes that she would elaborate, but nothing further was forthcoming. After a bit of patting my sister's back and saying "There, there" as comfortingly as I could manage, I asked, "What about Grandma? Tell me."

The result of my query was another outburst of emotion and an attempt to speak, but all I could understand was "Gra … Gr … Gr … she … she … she," followed by more uncontrollable crying. This was going nowhere, and my apprehension was growing. After some more back-patting and tut-tutting, I pulled away from the blubbering mass that was my sister and looked up into her face.

"Mands," I said, using Zac's nickname in the hopes that that would calm her down, "don't try to talk. Just listen to me and nod or shake your head, OK?"

She nodded.

"Good. Now, has something happened to Grandma?"

Another nod.

This next one was tough. "Is she dead?"

GG shook her head vehemently.

I closed my eyes. "Thank God." I loosened my grip on GG's lower arms: my fingers were starting to hurt. Who knows what it had felt like to her?

"OK," I said soothingly. "That's good news." Slowly I led her to the bed and sat her down, rolling up her desk chair so that I could face her.

"Mands, is Grandma in the hospital?"

"Yes," she sniveled.

Encouraged by the fact that my sibling had managed a coherent word, I asked a non-Yes-or-No question. "Can you tell me what happened?"

I got the story in tearful pieces, which I will put into comprehensible order.

The phone had rung in the middle of the night. GG had answered on the first ring, thinking it was Zac. Apparently 4 o'clock was their usual time. It was Mrs. Pelotti, Grandma's neighbor, a widow since her 20s who had always been extremely nice to us as children. (In fact, when Mands mentioned the name, I had an immediate craving for butterscotch, this being a favorite treat Mrs. Pelotti had always given us when we visited.) She had called to say that she'd been worried about Grandma, not having seen her all day, so she let herself in with the key Grandma had given her for just such emergencies.

She found Grandma on the bathroom floor, unconscious. Thinking it was a stroke, she checked for a pulse—weak, but steady—and called 911. The paramedics had taken her to the hospital, with Mrs. Pelotti following in her car. She was calling from the hospital, but she had no current information because she wasn't a relative.

GG had woken our parents, and they'd rushed off to the hospital, promising to call when they knew more. They hadn't called. As to why no one had bothered to tell me what was going on, I didn't ask and decided to confront my parents on the matter later, possibly during a visit to Dr. Feelgood.

I dialed both my parents' cell phone numbers, but Mother's immediately went to voice mail and Dad's rang from their bedroom.

GG didn't know which of the three Batshit hospitals they'd taken Grandma to, leaving us both feeling rather helpless. I went to my computer and looked up Mrs. Pelotti, but her number was unlisted. All we could do was wait.

The call never came. Instead, my dad's car pulled into the driveway shortly after 1 o'clock. By then Mandy and I were sitting on the couch, holding hands. I knew the news was not going to be good. Mother came in alone, which I assumed meant that Dad was at the funeral home making arrangements. Mother looked particularly grave, GG particularly apprehensive.

"What a morning!" Mother proclaimed, dropping her tired frame onto the sofa. Then, seeing how tense we were, "Didn't Dad call? Grandma's going to be fine."

"Dad left his cell phone here, Mother," I told her by way of an excuse.

"He still could have called," she remarked, but immediately thought the better of it. "He's in quite a state. Remember when his father died? He forgot *everything*."

"So what happened?" I asked. "How's Grandma?"

"Well, first things first: she didn't have a stroke," Mother told us. The relief was palpable; GG let go of my hand.

"So what was it?"

"Diabetic shock, apparently," Mother explained. "Thank God the paramedics caught the medical documents on her refrigerator. They knew she was taking insulin and guessed correctly from the outset that she'd taken too much."

[Aside: Mother was referring to the so-called Vial of Life Project. It involves putting all your medical information into a plastic bag, marking the bag with a special sticker and hanging it on the door of your refrigerator. Our town signed up for

the Vial of Life, and paramedics know to look for the bag of information. You can even put a second sticker on the door to your house to remind them to watch out for the bag. (And no, I have no idea why they call it a "vial.") At any rate, it's a very good system, as witnessed to by my grandmother. Check out the Project on the Internet and, if your town doesn't yet participate, badger them until they do.]

"But why would Grandma take too much? She wasn't trying to kill herself, was she?"

Mother let out a small laugh. "No, I don't think so. She's just getting old, Timothy. I talked to one of the nurses about it, and he told me that it happens a lot with old people. They aren't feeling well, think they might have forgotten their insulin and so they take it again without testing."

Out of the corner of my eye I noticed GG nodding her head. I looked and saw that she was focusing her eyes on Mother as she spoke. Mother noticed my surprise—I still have to work on my poker face—and gave me a little smile before continuing.

"The fact of the matter is, your grandmother never really understood her diabetes. She didn't get it till she was in her fifties, and she doesn't like dealing with it. She never watched her diet properly, and I don't think she tests herself very often either. She just gives herself the shots. Sometimes it's a little too much, sometimes not enough, sometimes just right, and she feels accordingly."

Mother paused while that sank in. If she was right, we had been fortunate up to now that there hadn't been more incidents of this kind.

"So where's Dad?" I asked.

"He's still at the hospital," Mother answered. "Talking to a social worker."

"A social worker? Why?"

"Well, Timothy, Mandy, that's what I wanted to talk to you about."

I looked at Mandy. Again, eyes focused, taking this all in.

"Your father and I agree that we can't leave Grandma on her own any more."

I felt my sister grabbing my hand.

"The doctors concur."

The squeeze on my hand grew tighter.

"We talked this morning about putting her in a home."

My hand was in real pain now. Mother mistook my tears as disapproval of this course of action.

"But that isn't the way we'd like to go."

Relief. GG eased her grip somewhat, and I could feel the blood returning to my fingers.

"We think it might be a good idea if Grandma moved in with us."

Silence.

"But we didn't want to do anything without talking to the two of you first."

Mandy withdrew her hand and drew a deep breath. I thought she might raise objections to the idea of a late addition to our family, but instead she simply nodded. "Fine," she said quietly.

Mother's smile wasn't only relief that her first-born was willing to go along with this life-changing decision. This was only the third time she had heard her daughter's voice in the better part of a year, and she rather liked the sound. She wisely refrained from commenting on it and looked at me.

"Timothy, what say you?"

"I say fine too," I said cheerily, for I was thinking it would be nice to have her around. "But do you think she'd be happy here? I mean, she's been at her house for over thirty years."

"Almost forty," Mother conceded. "And she's used to having a whole house. I don't think she'd be very happy in the guest room."

"Are you thinking of the fort, Mother?"

The fort was what we called one of Dad's long-abandoned projects. He had wanted to build an apartment above the garage to rent out so that the family would have a little more cash each month. This was when my parents first bought the house "on a shoestring," as they like saying, and they didn't know where the money was going to come from one month to the next.

The heating and plumbing were installed, and the drywall work was done. Essentially the apartment was a few weeks shy of being finished when Mother got her current job and our little family was suddenly, by comparison anyway, swimming in money. The project was abandoned, and the rooms above the garage became the place where Mandy had tea with her dollies and I fought off wild Indians back in those unenlightened, un-PC days.

"The fort is exactly what we were thinking about. Until it's ready, we thought we could get somebody to look in on her at her place. Mrs. Pelotti offered to help too."

"I think that's a great idea, Mother. And when Grandma can't handle the stairs any more, we can get one of those chair lifts."

"Good idea," Mother said. "Now all we have to do is convince your grandmother that that's the best thing to do."

"Grandpa's roses," I heard faintly from next to me.

Mother had perceived something, but she obviously couldn't make out what. "What was that?"

"Grandpa's roses," Mandy said, a little louder this time. Then, at full volume, "What about Grandpa's roses?" A complete sentence!

"What about them, dear?" Mother asked.

But GG had apparently said enough for one day, so I picked up where she left off. "Grandpa had the most beautiful roses, Mother."

"Yes, I remember." She sounded vaguely puzzled.

"And I ... *we* don't think Grandma will want to leave them behind."

GG nudged me in the side. I suspect it was meant to be gentle, but it nearly knocked the wind out of me.

"And Mandy and I would think it's a real shame too. Can we transplant them?"

"Oh, I see." She thought for a moment and said. "I don't see why not. I'd like to talk to a gardener first to find out if they'd survive the move, but yes, I like that idea."

Then, as if someone had flipped a switch, GG went back to her catatonic self, Mother disappeared upstairs to her room, and I fired up my game console. Dad was off somewhere else, and, except for the singing and praying crowd outside, it looked like any other Saturday at the Thompson residence.

Chapter 28

Not Just Another Sunday At The Thompsons'

Dad found a contractor that could start work on Grandma's new apartment that Monday. Mother was skeptical of a builder that was able to start work on such short notice, but apparently the owner showed Dad that the client on his current job had just filed for bankruptcy, thus explaining the lack of a wait.

"Now all I have to do is convince Grandma," Dad told us.

His mother could be quite stubborn at times, and she wasn't keen on giving up her independence. It was a bit of a risk to go ahead with the building work not knowing whether the tenant was even going to move in, but we all felt that, if we combined our efforts, Grandma would give in.

With the builder starting on Monday morning, GG and I had our work cut out for us: the fort needed to be emptied, and Sunday was our only chance to do it. At least to the fundamentalist hordes just outside our property line, Sunday was supposed to be a day of rest, but instead the praying protestors were privy to our family hard at work: GG and I hauling the detritus of years of our lives out of the garage; Dad slaving away at what, if the smell was any indication, was to be one of the finest meals he had ever put together; and Mother cleaning the house as if a) the Queen of England were coming and not a professor of biology, and b) Lucila, our Peruvian housekeeper, hadn't been there two days earlier. Mother's skillfully built image of a good Christian family was destroyed, at the very latest, when my sweet, Satanic sister started decapitating her old dolls in front of the gasping gawkers.

We managed to complete our various assigned chores by around 4 p.m. Mother decided the group out front needed another dose of her "Christian charity," as she called it, and made up more pots of cocoa and coffee, thinking it was probably too early in the day for mulled wine. (She did make some for herself afterwards, however.) But when the two of us went outside to divide the loaves and the fishes, as it were, there were noticeably fewer takers. I thought I heard someone whisper, "Who knows what's in it?" and then something like "witch's brew." I felt distinctly unwelcome in front of my own house.

I told Mother what I thought I'd heard as we went inside, but she just laughed. "No matter," she said. "At least I got a couple of them to agree to pray for Grandma while they're here. If *I* prayed for her, the Lord would probably take her now."

We all got cleaned up, and GG and I set the table. With all the excitement about Grandma, I'd forgotten to invite Megan, so there were going to be seven of us. I agonized over the best way to set the table for an odd number of diners for so long that GG went back to her room exasperated and put on some classic black metal music at full blast. I fully expected Mother to be upset, but she seemed delighted. I didn't understand why until she opened a window so that the gathering outside could partake of the obscenities, violent appeals to the Prince of Darkness and general misanthropic slurs. I will never understand my mother.

Mandy eventually turned off the music, and I heard her shower running for the second time. So she *was* planning to grace us with her presence and to try and make a good impression, no doubt for the sake of Zac. I finally finished the table, having opted for one place at either end, three on one side and two on the other. (The alternative, with one person at one end and three on either side, was, I decided after the third attempt to make it work, too formal.) The extra chair gave me pause, but in the end I decided to leave it in a corner, next to the sideboard.

My chores finished, I dared to take a look at the goings-on outside. I had expected the crowd to thin out after 6 o'clock, as people would be getting cold and hungry, but instead there were considerably more people gathered than in the afternoon. I estimated that there were about fifty Christian soldiers out there, and more were arriving by car even as I watched. Each person was given a candle as they arrived, and I saw that Mrs. McDermitt was the one doing the honors of lighting them. The candles cast some eerie shadows, and an image of villagers storming the castle to torch it came into my head.

The image was startled out of me by a loud knock at the back door. I assumed Dad had locked himself out while taking out the garbage, so I was more than a little surprised to see Zac there. I let him in and was even more shocked at his appearance. I'm not entirely sure what I'd been expecting, but certainly not this!

Zac was, as my grandmother was wont to put it, dressed to the nines. He hadn't departed from his basic black, which I utterly respected. He had chosen a blazer, a proper shirt, dress pants and sensible leather shoes. His belt was fashionably narrow, the belt buckle simple. And not a pentagram in sight! His hair was neatly combed, though the discerning could readily recognize that he normally wore it in spikes. He wore only a trace of makeup around the eyes, and it was surprisingly tastefully done. I was truly impressed and immediately wondered what my sister would be wearing to the soirée.

"Hey, Zac," I greeted him. "You look really nice."

"Thanks, man. But just so you know: I don't swing that way."

"Duly noted," I said crisply. Then, almost as an afterthought, "Me neither."

"Oh, OK. I just thought …"

"That's all right. It seems to be a common mistake. Come on into the living-room," I suggested. "Why did you come the back way?"

"Have you looked outside lately? Even in my Sunday best, I don't think that's my crowd."

"Yeah," I chuckled. "I see what you mean. And the crowd's been growing."

"Maybe they got word that Cyrus Abrams is coming."

"I don't see how," I said, but at that moment I suddenly did see: I had mentioned it to Mr. Powers, and his secretary was obviously one of the organizers of the protest. There was no more room for the benefit of the doubt: she was definitely eavesdropping on my conversations with her boss!

Zac and I enjoyed some small talk for a few minutes before "Mands" came down the stairs. I was amazed, and Zac clearly liked what he saw too. GG was wearing a black-and-white ensemble: a white blouse with a black vest, a black skirt and low-heeled shoes. Instead of her usual black fishnet stockings, she wore nylons with wide, horizontal, black-and-white stripes, which didn't look as comical as they probably sound. The spiked leather dog collar was a subtle reminder of who she was, but it didn't destroy the classy look. (I suspect that was because it was fairly narrow, at least in relation to her massive neck.) She had avoided makeup, as far as I could tell, but she didn't seem quite as pale as usual, which I attributed to the hard work we had done in the garage all day: that sort of thing gets the blood flowing. Even her lips looked vaguely pinkish—a startling shock of color which she normally kept hidden under black lipstick.

Clearly Zac and GG had conspired to tone down their otherwise aggressive appearance for the sake of Cyrus Abrams, but they had done so without denying who they were. I wanted to compliment GG on the new style, but Zac beat me to it.

"Wow," was all he said, and his word had the surprising effect of tickling a smile out of my big sister. I nodded at her as a sign of assent, and she seemed to appreciate the gesture, even from her geeky little brother.

Only then did I notice that Zac was very early. Dad had told him to come at 7, yet it was only 6:30. I remarked on it and Zac explained.

"Your dad called and said he wanted me to come at 6:30 instead of 7. I guess I'm going to get the third degree before the other guests get here."

"Something like that." It was Dad, who had come downstairs and managed to sneak up on us. "Son, why don't you go up to your room and get ready?"

"I am ready," I said innocently, then, catching Dad's drift, I mumbled that maybe I could put on a different shirt.

"Why don't you come and help me in the kitchen, Zac?" I heard as I headed for the stairs. "We can talk and work at the same time."

The interrogation can't have been so bad, as both Dad and the young Goth were smiling when they emerged twenty minutes later. I was relieved: if Zac had had to leave before dinner, I'd have had to reset the table.

Mother came downstairs at precisely seven o'clock, dressed casually but elegantly. She took in the way her daughter and friend presented themselves, and her relief was palpable. "Hello, Zac. Nice to finally meet you," she said graciously, offering him her hand.

For a second I was worried he might kiss it, but he clearly came from a household where people knew how to behave themselves. He shook her hand briefly and firmly, but without exerting pressure, as I could see from a micro-expression on Mother's face: she was impressed.

"Our other guests haven't arrived yet?" she asked.

"It's seven on the dot, Ronnie," Dad said.

We all sat down in the living-room for some chit-chat, which went astoundingly well. It was just after 7:15 when Mother wondered out loud whether we should be worried about Professor Abrams and his daughter, but even as she spoke, the doorbell rang. I went to the door while the others waited.

Professor Abrams looked exactly like his pictures, and very professorial: slightly tousled, curly brown hair with graying temples, round glasses, a tan, corduroy jacket with leather patches at the elbows, a black turtleneck sweater, crisp, black jeans and Hush Puppies™. One could even say he looked like the caricature of a university professor; the only thing missing was the pipe between his teeth.

Miss Abrams was looking uncharacteristically radiant, which I came to realize over the course of the evening was a by-product of being around her father. The two obviously had an excellent rapport, and though Miss Abrams evidently admired her father, she was not in any way in awe of him. Their banter was playful and affectionate, and there was teasing from both sides. I have noted that families in which there is a great deal of good-natured teasing are generally quite harmonious and content.

After the Abramses got settled and the introductions had been made, Professor Abrams began by apologizing for their tardiness. "I can assure you we weren't trying to be fashionably late," he joked. "But it was practically impossible to get a parking spot around here."

Dad jumped in. "It's not usually like this. But as I'm sure you noticed, we're drawing quite a crowd here."

"The welcoming committee?" Miss Abrams remarked. "Yes, we noticed."

"They didn't harass you, did they?" Mother asked, concerned that her guests might have been ill treated.

"No more than usual," the professor said.

"Get a lot of that, do you?" Dad said.

"Pretty much everywhere I go. This is the first time I've been greeted by 'When the Saints Go Marching in' though. I felt flattered."

We all had a laugh, Zac a tad too loudly.

"The sit-down blockade was a new one for me," Miss Abrams interjected.

"Oh, didn't I tell you? They're doing that everywhere now," the professor explained. He looked around to lock eyes with each of us, and we paid him rapt attention. "You see, these groups are very well organized on a national scale. And well-financed."

"Who would give money to people just so they can get in your way?" Zac asked.

"You'd be surprised," the professor answered.

"Cyrus," Dad interrupted, "excuse me. If you don't mind holding off your answer for a few minutes, I'd like to serve dinner. Can we head over to the dining room?"

Once we got settled in, the good professor surprised us all. "Do you mind if I say grace?"

"Not at all," my mother said. "Be my guest."

Cyrus Abrams began, "Lord, thank you for allowing the seven of us to be here today in this lovely home. Thank you for providing for us so generously. And thank you for the opportunity to speak tomorrow so that I can spread the word about the wonders of evolution."

"Amen," said Miss Abrams, and with a slight delay, the rest of us.

After a moment of dignified silence, I spoke. "Professor? I'm curious."

Our famous guest smiled. "Why I believe in God?"

"Yes. I mean, I think I believe in God, but I'm not sure I know why. And you, as a scientist, ..."

"... should be an atheist," he completed my sentence.

"Well, yes. I mean, Steven Hawking has written that the origins of the universe can be explained without God."

"I'm not an astrophysicist, but Professor Hawking is probably correct. We don't *need* God to explain anything."

"So why do you think he exists?" This came from Mandy, to my family's surprise.

"Faith," was his simple reply. "I believe it was Clarence Darrow who said, 'I do not pretend to know where many ignorant men are sure.' But I have this deep, inner conviction that he is there. Of course he's nothing like the God the good people freezing their butts off out there believe in, but I do believe there's a Supreme Being.

"I wouldn't dream of proselytizing. I'm not even sure what my own daughter here believes in, if anything."

Miss Abrams laughed. "I believe my dad is just hedging his bets." Noticing the blank looks around the table, she explained further. "I don't think he really believes in God, but just in case, he's paying his respects to the man upstairs. That way he can't lose: if there's no God, no harm done; if there *is* a God, Dad can tell St. Peter up at the pearly gates that he was a believer."

We all had a good laugh and continued to enjoy Dad's amazing baked pear appetizer. Professor Abrams picked up his train of thought from earlier.

"Ah, but we were talking about something else before. Oh right, financing." He speared a succulent piece of pear and savored it. "This is delicious, by the way, Paul." Then to Zac: "Now, young man, you asked who the backers of the creationists are. Well, there are many, but in our neck of the woods, the Discovery Institute and two rather wealthy businessman brothers seem to be most active."

I noted that Mother seemed to know whom he was referring to.

"Are you saying the protesters out there are being paid to do it?" I ventured.

"No, no. Those are good but seriously misguided people who would do anything for what they think is God's will. The financing goes to the organizational effort, ad campaigns, lobbying and legal fees. Hundreds of millions per year, by my reckoning."

Dad whistled his surprise. "Hundreds of millions? That's incredible."

"Yes," the professor said, "my old granny would have to knit a lot of sweaters to get that kind of money."

"But why?" Dad asked. "I mean, what's their angle? It's not like there's money to be made."

"It's all about politics, Paul." This came from Mother. "Fundamentalist Christians can be relied on to support all kinds of conservative causes."

"I don't get it," I said.

"Your mother is quite right, Timothy," Professor Abrams said. "A mailing list of fundamentalist Christians is worth its weight in gold to conservatives. People who feel strongly about creationism probably have strong feelings about other issues as well, and they can be manipulated into taking action. If you can convince them that what you want is God's will, they'll do just about anything for you."

"Can you give us an example, Professor?" Zac pitched in.

"Gladly. Let's say that you're a conservative, and you're trying to prevent a gun control bill from passing Congress. You know you have your work cut out for you: after all, most Americans want more, not less, gun control."

"You'd never know that from reading the papers or watching TV news!" Dad exclaimed.

"Exactly!" our illustrious guest said. "Because the gun lobby is where the money is. But how to convince Congress? Well," the good professor said, answering his own question, "get a few hundred thousand people to write to their congressmen and senators, that's how."

"Oh, I get it now," I said. "That's where the mailing list comes in. You write to everybody on the list telling them God wants them to write to their congressman opposing gun control."

"That's exactly right, Timothy. The Christian groups are among the best organized in the nation, and more people on their mailing lists will comply and write those emails and letters than in any other group."

"So it's one huge lobbying organization," Dad summed up.

"And a very effective one at that. No other organization can flood Congress with more letters in support of or in opposition to a pending bill than they can."

"So are you saying the whole creationist thing is a ruse?" Zac speculated.

"No, I suspect not," Cyrus Abrams replied. "I'm pretty sure most of the people campaigning and pushing the creationist agenda are sincere. The rest is a by-product and the reason they get financial backing."

Conversation moved on from there to politics in general (main course), then to the state of education in America (also main course), to our school in particular (dessert). With Mother's help I filled Professor Abrams in on the details his daughter hadn't provided him.

"The strange thing is," Mother said, "I get the impression that Mrs. Barker was actually disappointed that this whole sordid affair never came to trial."

"Hmm," the professor said, "she may well be a plant. It wouldn't be the first time."

"Now who's fueling the conspiracy theories?" Miss Abrams asked. The remark apparently harked back to some earlier conversation I know nothing of.

"Now, Emily," her father scolded, "it's not all that unlikely. Veronica just explained that this point of law has never been clarified: can a teacher be forced to teach something he or she doesn't believe in? So it doesn't seem so unlikely that some fundamentalist group put Mrs. Barker here to try and force a lawsuit."

"The precedent would have been devastating," Mother pointed out. "If they had won, it would have meant teachers could teach whatever they wanted, the state curriculum be damned."

"Not only that," the famous professor added, "it would have allowed local groups to put enormous pressure on science teachers."

"How do you mean, Professor?" Zac asked.

"Think about it. Today science teachers can rely on the state curriculum in their defense if parents or anybody else tries to pressure them not to teach evolution. They can tell the pressure groups, 'Sorry, but I *have* to teach this—it's in the state standards for biology.' But what if those standards were no longer requirements? What if the courts hollowed them out to the point that they were mere recommendations?

"We could be looking at a whole new tactic here: first the creationists tried to get equal time with evolution, and the courts consistently said no, creationism is religion and doesn't belong in the public schools. Then they tried to sneak in creationism under a different name, intelligent design. That didn't work either, so now they're trying something new.

"Essentially, they're saying, 'If we can't teach creationism in public schools, we're going to make it so difficult for teachers to teach evolution that they won't want to.' I mean, how many teachers are going to stand up and defy a well-organized bunch of parents who don't want evolution taught if they don't have a curriculum *requirement* to hide behind? It would be much easier to simply leave out that chapter and avoid the confrontation."

"Ingenious," Mother said.

"Diabolical," said GG.

An uncomfortable silence ensued that the guest of honor finally broke. "So tell me, Timothy, what are the arrangements for tomorrow?"

Everyone except GG, who had not noticed the brief lull in the conversation, expressed their gratitude with a perceptible and simultaneous sigh. I then went on to explain to the professor when he was expected, whom he would be meeting, ultimately telling him that I would be introducing him. I checked the details of Professor Abrams' distinguished career that I intended to use in my introduction—I never completely trust online sources, and many a contradiction was to be found about the man.

Things slowed down after that as our guests prepared to leave. The ritual offer to help with the cleanup was made, the ritual refusal given. Good-byes were said, hands shaken.

Somehow the crowd outside—who we had all completely forgotten about—seemed to sense that the main object of their Christian hatred was on the move, and they struck up yet another round of "Rock of Ages."

"Professor," Zac offered, "there's a back way out of here. I'd be happy to show you." When Cyrus Abrams appeared to be thinking about it, Zac added, "Guaranteed protestor-free" as an enticement.

"Thanks for the offer, Zac," the professor said, "but I prefer to confront those who would seek to persecute me." (I later looked up Professor Abrams' slightly bizarre choice of words and found out that "seek to persecute" is used in the Bible, but also apparently in the Quran and quite extensively in the labor movement and other progressive causes.)

As Professor and Miss Abrams stepped out the door with Zac, the singing grew louder, and some of the protesters started to sit down on the cold ground so as to be in the way of our guests as they headed for their car.

I would like to be able to say that I witnessed with my own eyes what happened next, but I was carrying dishes into the kitchen when I heard a commotion. From what I heard during the incident and from my parents talking to the police later, this is what happened.

A man nobody knew or even noticed before stepped out of the crowd toward Professor and Miss Abrams, produced a handgun from his coat pocket and pointed it at the professor's head. He shouted something, but all I could make out was "Die, infidel!" Others claimed it was "Die, heathen!" but they, of course, were wrong.

I also clearly heard Mrs. McDermitt scream out "He's got a gun," but from my vantage point in the dining-room I was unable to discern what anyone else said amidst all the screaming and shouting.

The exact order of what happened next will never be conclusively determined, as witness accounts differ, but the most plausible explanation for what I saw when I finally arrived on the scene is that Zac grabbed and twisted the man's arm, a diminutive Christian (in the best sense of the word) woman from the crowd started beating the gunman on the back, while my dad flew off our front stoop and tackled the would-be assassin before he could get off a shot.

The man did manage to fire his weapon, which he still held firmly in his hand while my dad and Zac were pressing his face into our front lawn, but the single shot that sounded hit nothing: the projectile was never retrieved.

Professor Abrams remained calm throughout the entire ordeal. In fact, he seemed more upset about the fuss being made than about the attempt on his life. When I offered to release him from his commitment to speak the next day, he would have none of it.

The police interviews went on into the wee hours, and the flashing lights from their cars also did their part to prevent my getting more than three hours of sleep before the big day.

Chapter 29

The Circus Comes To Town

It is impossible to say whether the national press would have covered the evolution lectures at all, much less so thoroughly, had there not been an attempted assassination of our keynote speaker. I am not a great one for "What if"-games, so the question is, in the end, immaterial. At any rate, by the Monday morning when the presentations were to begin, every American news organization I had ever heard of was present in Batshit.

My first indication that that particular Monday was going to be different came when I went downstairs and turned on the TV in the kitchen. My parents and I like to watch the news while having breakfast. (It is unclear whether GG also likes it.) As the picture appeared on-screen, I saw a house not unlike our own featured quite prominently. I did a double-take as I saw the camera zooming in toward one of the windows and saw: myself! There I was, standing in front of the television set, staring at the front and side of my house on TV. The one- to two-second delay as the signal was beamed from the news station truck to a satellite, only to be beamed to the station itself a mere four miles away, made the situation all the more surreal.

I turned toward the window and saw several broadcasting trucks and a gaggle of reporters, some talking into cameras while holding improbably large microphones, gathered on the street. Only then did I become aware that my old pajamas with prints of antique cars were perhaps not the most suitable attire for a national television appearance and that they might lead to a certain amount of ridicule at school later. I drew the blinds and then went upstairs to shower and change, listening as I did so to a report about the previous evening's attack on Cyrus Abrams.

With the entire family assembled around the breakfast table, we zapped our way through all the channels that carried news at breakfast time. We watched our neighbors leaving for work and being hassled by reporters for inside information on the family at our address: "no comment—now get out of my way!" We saw interviews with supposed eye witnesses to the attempt on our guest's life: "a large knife—more like a machete—and a sawed-off shotgun." We heard from a local pastor we did not know and had, in fact, never heard of as he passed judgment on our family: "basically good people, but spiritually misguided."

One of the more interesting interviews—most of which we missed—was with Mrs. McDermitt and Mrs. Barker. They clearly distanced themselves from any and all violent activity and called it "un-Christian." They stated unequivocally that they had their beliefs, and that others were entitled to theirs, however wrong they might be in God's eyes. In fact, the pair sounded like the voice of reason, except of course for the fact that they said they communicated with God directly and that He had created the world and all life on it as it is today "less than 10,000 years ago."

"Good for them," my dad commented. And then he made a heretical suggestion: "Shall we have a look what the 'F' people are making of all this?" Much to my surprise, Mother consented with, I hasten to add, enthusiasm.

"Oh yes, let's," she said.

The 'F' word in our house is not the same word as it is elsewhere. Instead this distinction is reserved for a certain ultra-conservative "news" network whose viewers are consistently ranked as the nation's most misinformed individuals. Our local affiliate happens to be Channel 6, but it has been relegated to another spot on our TV remote: 666. (For those who are unfamiliar with the significance of these numbers: "666" is the sign of Satan.) Dad clicked in just as the announcer was transitioning from some sort of fuzzy animal "report" to the news we were most interested in.

As on all the serious news channels, the report opened with a shot of our house. The prose that accompanied the picture was, for lack of a better description, purple: "This quiet, leafy suburban street in Batshit, Illinois, witnessed a brutal attack late last night on the noted evolution propagandist Cyril Abrahams. Police say a mentally disturbed individual pulled a gun on the noted professor as he left the home of radical attorney Veronica Langley-Thompson with a female companion who F** News will not identify due to long-standing network policy protecting minors.

"According to eye-witness accounts of the incident, Professor Abrahams was saved by a young male Satanist who was also accompanying the anti-Christian activist. We'll have more after the break."

"I don't think I'm up for 'more after the break,'" radical attorney Veronica Langley-Thompson said.

"Mother, can we sue them?" I asked.

"For mispronouncing 'Batshit' or for getting Professor Abrams' name wrong?"

"You know what I mean, Mother," I said somewhat testily.

"Well, this is America, Timothy. You can sue anybody."

"I was referring more to the tendentious characterizations. Calling you a 'radical attorney' or implying that Professor Abrams is a pedophile. I mean, Miss Abrams is not a minor."

Mother immediately went into her lawyerly mode. "Freedom of speech goes pretty far, Timothy. Most of what they said can be chalked up to matters of opinion, which are not actionable. And even if we could sue them, the most we could possibly expect is a correction. My professional advice? Don't bother. Now can you change the channel, Paul, before I have to throw up?"

Dad did her one better and clicked off the TV. We finished breakfast in silence. After I'd gathered my books and things for school, the doorbell rang.

"If that's a reporter," Mother shouted from upstairs, "shoot him!"

No shooting was necessary. It was Mike Petersson at the door. "Hi, Timothy," he grinned. "I thought you could maybe use some help getting through the crowd."

"How did you know?" I asked him.

"Duh" and a nod toward the TV were his only responses. Then with a chuckle, "Nice jammies, by the way."

With the imposing figure of Mike next to me, the reporters blocking our path parted like the Red Sea for Moses. A few started to follow us, but Mike simply turned around and cast them a look that was gauged to kill any lesser mortal. They decided that retreat was the better part of valor and stayed put, possibly in the hopes of juicier—and easier—prey.

I figured there would be more reporters outside the school, but nothing could have prepared me for the sight that awaited us. It wasn't just reporters, though they were there in numbers.

Batshitians were out in force, as well as countless outsiders. The first group we saw were the crazies from Westboro Baptist Church, the ones who generally picket the funerals of fallen soldiers with signs that read "God hates America" and "God hates fags." They apparently were not so well connected that they recognized Mike and me upon our approach, so we got only the earful of anti-homosexual rhetoric everyone else was treated to. We were also informed that we were doomed.

"Buncha nuts" was all Mike had to say about them.

Separated from the Westboro group by a small contingent of state police was a single organ grinder with his pet monkey. It took a few moments for the penny to drop, but then I understood the (tenuous) connection to the day's events: evolution lectures, monkeys. As if to dispel any doubt I may have had about the connection, when we came closer I saw that the monkey was wearing a little suit and hat. A sign around its neck read, "Say hi to Grandpa." Clever? Clever enough to attract several TV cameras and throngs of people waiting to put money into a tin can mounted in front of the organ grinder.

The organ grinder was obviously thought to be neither a threat nor endangered, so only one local policeman watched over him. The next group showed considerable overlap with the crowd outside our house over the weekend: God-fearing and probably harmless Christians. They were under somewhat closer scrutiny: ten local police and Mrs. McDermitt observed their activities. It was clear from the expression on Mrs. McDermitt's face that she would only allow people she knew to participate in the vigil, as she did not want a repeat of last night's incident.

Mrs. McDermitt's group was, as usual, singing, and I must admit that they had improved considerably over the course of the weekend. Everyone seemed more or less on key, and perhaps more significantly, they all knew the words to the hymn, which I was unfamiliar with. I expected them to get louder (or worse) as Mike and I passed, but instead several members of the group broke ranks and approached us with extended hands to shake and express apology and/or consolation. I found the gesture touching, but it clearly made my bodyguard nervous.

Getting closer to the school's main entrance, we passed a group of people in lab coats handing out leaflets showing an evolution timeline. A sign identified them as "Christian health practitioners for the teaching of evolution," which was apparently an ad hoc group for the show of solidarity in Batshit because I couldn't find them on the Internet. I recognized one of the women as my dental hygienist and said hello.

Mike and I made it to the entrance where, much to our surprise, all doors but the one at the far right were locked and labeled "closed" with large red and white signs. Behind the far right door stood an airport-style security gateway which we had to pass through. I know that metal detectors are used in some urban schools, but this was a first for Omar L. Batshit High School, and I wondered whether this had been planned all along or was added as an extra precaution after the attack on Cyrus Abrams.

"There he is," I heard from down the hall. "The young man who made all this possible."

I took the remark for sarcasm at best, but then I realized the voice belonged to Mr. Powers, who was smiling as broadly as I've ever seen a human being smile. As he approached, I was shocked: he looked 30 years younger!

"Remember our little talk, Timothy?" the principal said. "This is what education is all about!"

Finally Mr. Powers took note of the hulk by my side. "Mr. Petersson, good to see you. A fine match last week, a fine match."

"Thank you, Mr. Powers, sir," Mike said, slightly overwhelmed by the warm greeting and especially the recognition from a man whom, he told me later, he had never spoken to personally and had, in fact, up to that point feared.

"I hear your hard work with Timothy here is paying off," the still beaming old man exclaimed. "Positively stellar. Now if you'll excuse me, I need to abscond with your tutor."

Mr. Powers' enthusiasm was effusive. Looking out the window of his office at the crowds below, he exclaimed, "Here we have it, Timothy. Passion! People are getting passionate about something being taught at this school. Look at them!"

I did look, and I was surprised to see so many students engaging with the various groups outside. True, the organ grinder and his monkey were drawing the biggest crowd, but some of my fellow students were talking—in some cases heatedly—with the demonstrators. I could see the principal's point.

"Ah, but we must get down to business," Mr. Powers said. "How is our guest doing after last night's unpleasantness?"

"I haven't spoken to him today, but he was remarkably calm about the whole thing yesterday," I explained. "And he said he definitely wants to speak to us today."

"Excellent," Mr. Powers said, "excellent. As you have witnessed, the police are taking precautions that no weapons enter the plant. What sort of impression would Professor Abrams get of our little burgh if another fanatic were to take up arms against him? Not to mention the effect the publicity is having for our community."

"Yes, I wasn't expecting national news stations to be here," I said with dread.

"Indeed. The mayor has been on the blower to me twice this morning. That's twice more than he has contacted me since being elected."

"Presumably he isn't happy about the publicity?" I ventured.

"In the first call he was exceedingly happy. 'This will put Batshit on the map,' he told me. When I reminded him that someone could have lost a life, he was slightly less exuberant, but he was quite excited that we were getting our fifteen minutes of fame.

"Twenty minutes later, when he rang again, his tune had changed. Apparently some of the reporters had been making jokes about the name of our fair community and begun using terms like 'backwater town' and 'local yokels' when reporting on the creationist/evolution controversy that brought us here in the first place.

"I quoted, of course, the old adage that there's no such thing as *bad* publicity, but he was not convinced. For the sake of your young ears, I won't relay his words verbatim, but suffice it to say he was unhappy."

"Backwater?" I protested. "That's not fair. Something like 40% of Americans believe in the biblical version of creation. It's not just the 'local yokels'!"

"You're right, of course, but exercising media critique will get us precisely nowhere.—Back to Professor Abrams. When he gets here, I'd like you to greet him and bring him here, to my office, for a chat. I've taken the liberty of advising your teachers for the morning that you will not be present in their lessons."

"Thank you, Mr. Powers," I said. It was a phy ed day, and I knew Coach Braun would not be pleased. I apparently have a talent for making people unhappy.

Mr. Powers wanted to know all about the attack on Professor Abrams, and he was disappointed to learn that I hadn't witnessed it myself. A few minutes before 9 o'clock, when our guest speaker was expected, I went to the main entrance to greet him. He and Miss Abrams were just approaching the door when I arrived.

"That's quite a welcome you've prepared for me," Professor Abrams said, motioning toward the swelling crowd outside. Most of them looked less than friendly, and I noticed that another busload of policemen was pulling up. This thing was getting huge.

"Is it always like this?" I asked the professor as I accompanied him and Miss Abrams to Principal Powers' office.

"Actually, this is the biggest anti-evolution rally I've seen."

"Sorry about that," I apologized. "This isn't how I expected it to be."

"Don't worry, Timothy," Miss Abrams said. "My dad likes it this way."

"You can't educate them unless you draw them out," the professor added.

Mr. Powers, who was waiting in the hall outside his office, heard and said, "I couldn't agree more, Professor. Jonathan Powers—pleased to meet you."

"The pleasure's all mine," our guest announced. "You, sir, are the stuff of legend."

"Don't believe a word of it," Mr. Powers said.

Miss Abrams looked almost as puzzled as I was, and her father answered the implied query. "You may not be aware that Jonathan Powers is one of the most influential education reformers in the state, if not the country."

"I don't know about the influential part," Mr. Powers protested modestly. "One of the most vociferous, perhaps, but our schools would look very different today if I were truly influential. Very different."

"Point taken," conceded Professor Abrams. "So, what are the plans for this morning's festivities?"

Before the principal could answer, I interrupted politely and asked to be excused. I wanted to check that the auditorium was ready for the expected onslaught. The third period was starting in just under an hour, and with it our two-hour program.

When I entered the auditorium I noted that everything seemed to be in place. Ms. Pewney, as faculty advisor to all things drama, including the auditorium technical crew, was just doing a last-minute light check.

"I said stage left, Brandon, left," Ms. Pewney screamed into the darkness at the rear of our school's state-of-the-art theater.

"Sorry" came the echo out of the darkness, and the lights came on stage left.

"That's more like it," my English teacher praised. Then catching sight of me, "Timothy, hello. Are you here to check up on us? I think we're ready—if Brandon can remember the difference between left and right, that is." She mumbled the last sentence so that only I could hear.

"I'm sure everything will be fine," I said, then strode toward the stage. Climbing the stairs, I noted that there was one more chair than I'd specified.

I called down to Ms. Pewney: "I see there's an extra chair. Did Josh Curtin decide to show his face after all?"

"No, Mr. Powers wants to be on stage with Mr. Grass and the Science Club," she answered. Approaching the stage she said, again more quietly, "As for Josh—you haven't heard?"

I felt as if someone had punched me in the stomach. Something had happened to my best, though often irritating, friend. "What's wrong? What happened to Josh?" I asked breathlessly.

By this time Ms. Pewney had climbed onto the stage. "Nothing has happened to Josh," she said. "It's his father."

I felt guilty at my own relief. "Oh, nothing serious, I hope."

"Actually," said Ms. Pewney hesitantly, "he's been arrested."

"Arrested? Why?"

I had only met Josh's dad once and seen him from a distance a few times when he had come to pick up Josh from school, but I knew that his parents were church-going folk, not criminals.

"Well," she hedged, "the man who attacked Cyrus Abrams outside your house last night …"

I couldn't believe where this was going.

"… was Josh's father. Apparently he belongs to some radical Christian sect, and he went crazy when he heard that the famous promoter of evolution and other such heresy was going to be speaking in his hometown—at his son's school, no less. And he tried to shoot him."

For the second time in the span of a few minutes I felt a blow to my mid-section. I grabbed the back of one of the chairs that had been positioned for the panel discussion that was to follow Professor Abrams' talk, then eased myself into it. Ms. Pewney put her hand on my shoulder.

"I'm sorry you had to find out like this, Timothy." She offered me some water from the pitcher that was already in place for the panel. "Drink this—you'll feel better."

It took me several minutes to recover, but I eventually forced myself to get up and finish my last-minute check-up. Seeing the beautifully carved lectern—a gift of the Class of '73, according to the plaque—I decided to adjust the microphone, since I would be the first person to speak when I introduced Professor Abrams.

Walking toward the lectern, I gratefully registered that someone had placed a small stoop behind it. The lectern was rather high, and I'd been concerned that I might not be able to look over the top of it. Stepping onto the stoop, I noticed that it gave way and emitted a clear clicking sound, as if some sort of mechanism had been engaged.

At first I found it merely odd that someone had designed a stoop for short people to stand behind the lectern without looking silly, only to have the platform give way slightly though measurably. Then my thoughts flashed to a film I'd watched from my parents' DVD collection: *Lethal Weapon 2*.

Though not great cinema, *Lethal Weapon 2* is an action-packed and at times very funny movie. My favorite scene involves Danny Glover sitting down on a toilet and activating a bomb. Getting up would cause the bomb to explode and most assuredly kill him. Somehow I felt that I might have stepped onto a similar trap. As inconceivable as that scenario would have been less than 24 hours earlier, the attempted murder in my own front yard made me reluctant to rule it out.

"Ms. Pewney," I called, somewhat tentatively. "Could you come here, please?"

She was talking to two stage hands in the middle of the auditorium. "I'm rather busy, Timothy. I'd rather you came here."

"I really need you to come here," I said.

There must have been desperation in my voice because she immediately broke off her conversation and rushed toward the stage. "What is it?" she asked, with a mixture of annoyance and concern.

"Do you know who put this stoop here that I'm standing on?"

"What stoop?" she asked, heading up the stairs to the stage again. Then, seeing what I meant, she said, "No, it wasn't us. Why?"

"Well, when I got on it, it went down about half an inch, and there was a metallic click."

"And you're thinking IED?" Ms. Pewney asked matter-of-factly.

"I don't know what IED is," I said. "I'm thinking land-mine."

Getting down onto her knees with considerable grace for a woman of her height, she said, as if we were back in her classroom, "An IED, Timothy, is an improvised explosive device. They're used by insurgents in asymmetrical warfare, which is when one side is militarily greatly superior to the other."

"You seem to know a lot about these things," I said, "for an English teacher."

"We all have a past, Timothy," she said, now trying to peer into the stoop. Then she shouted to her technicians, "Lights on full, center stage!"

The command "center stage" seemed to present far less of a problem for Brandon, for the lights went up immediately.

Ms. Pewney cranked her head around, still trying to see into the stoop at my feet. "Hmm," she said. "I don't like the looks of that."

"What? What do you see?" I was starting to panic.

"Don't worry, Timothy, but you may be right about that stoop," she said. "There's something inside it—I did *not* say a bomb—but why would anyone build a stoop with *anything* inside? Just stay put."

"OK," I said meekly. "Shouldn't we call the police?"

"I'd rather not until we know for sure, Timothy." Then loudly, to her technicians, "One of you bring me the toolbox, please."

An attractive girl I'd seen a few times around school came with the toolbox. "Here you are, Ms. P.," she said. Then, staring disbelievingly at the sight of a teacher in a charcoal-gray dress lying on the floor poking at a wooden box with a screwdriver, "What are you doing?"

"Just a few last-minute adjustments, dear," Ms. Pewney answered sweetly. "Now, Rebecca, I want you and the others to get out of here and go straight to Principal Powers. Go to him only, and tell him that Vince Lombardi is in the auditorium. Do you understand?"

The poor girl looked around, obviously puzzled, since there was no one else in the auditorium but the three of us and three more technicians in the back. And if she knew that Vince Lombardi had been the head coach of the Green Bay Packers in the 1950s and '60s, she was probably even more confused.

"I don't understand, Ms. P.," she said. "Vince who?"

"Vince Lombardi," the teacher repeated slowly. "It's very important, Rebecca. And remember, tell no one but Mr. Powers."

Rebecca sounded skeptical, but she agreed to do as she was told. Once we were alone in the auditorium, I asked, "Am I right that 'Vince Lombardi' is code for a bomb?"

"I just saw a wire in there, Timothy. So please try and stand still for a while more."

"I'll do my best, Ms. Pewney," I said, starting to shiver. "Shouldn't you get out of here, just in case?"

"No, no," she said merrily. "I'm not going to let some silly little bomb scare me away from a chance to talk to my prize student."

Most incongruously, Ms. Pewney began to discuss *The Red Badge of Courage* with me, with particular emphasis on the symbolism of the squirrel. I was just about to offer my theories on that when Mr. Powers' voice came over the PA system.

"Ladies and gentlemen," he began. "Due to a problem with one of the boilers in the heating plant, the fire department has asked us to evacuate the premises immediately. This is a precautionary measure, so there's no need for panic. But please move quickly out onto the football field behind the school. Stay with your current class groups—attendance will be taken. I know it's cold out there, but to paraphrase Vince Lombardi, the legendary football coach, your body can stand most anything. It's your mind you have to convince. So think warm thoughts and get moving."

Ms. Pewney chuckled. "Not the best Lombardi quote I've heard, but pretty good on the spur of the moment. Now the teachers will make sure the school is completely evacuated."

"And then what?" I asked.

"And then we're going to disarm the bomb under your feet."

"We?"

"Well, somebody has to do it," she said. "By the way, do you know how 'Vince Lombardi' came to be the code word for a bomb in our school?"

"Erm, no."

"That was my idea. We were having a faculty meeting a few years ago where we had to agree on code words for all sorts of emergencies," Ms. Pewney explained, though I was barely listening. It was obvious to me that she was merely trying to distract my attention from the fact that I was about to be torn to shreds by an IED.

"Anyway," she continued, "I had just read that someone was planning to produce a play on Broadway about Vince Lombardi's life … or career … or some such nonsense. Now anyone who knows Broadway can tell you that sports dramas don't sell tickets—they *bomb*. So I suggested 'Vince Lombardi' as the code word, and much to my surprise, Coach Braun picked up on it immediately. I mean, it effectively meant that we could never talk about Vince Lombardi in school, unless of course there was a bomb threat. A shooting spree, on the other hand, would …"

I was saved from this verbal barrage by Mr. Powers' voice, only this time he was physically present in the auditorium. "What have we got, Ms. Pewney?" he shouted from the back.

"It seems our friend Timothy here has stepped onto a pressure-sensitive IED. If I'm correct, it is rigged to go off as soon as the pressure is released. Have you notified the police?"

"Yes," the old man said, "that's why I'm here. It appears that Timothy couldn't have chosen a worse time to step onto this device."

I wasn't sure if this was meant as actual criticism, or whether the comment was sardonic. I chose not to react.

"There is some sort of law enforcement convention in Las Vegas, and the Batshit bomb squad, which, I am told, consists of one man, is there. It will take at least another hour for someone to get here from the capital. Can you hold out that long, Timothy?"

"I don't know, Mr. Powers," I said. Then, trying to sound brave, I added, "I'll try."

"The alternative," Mr. Powers said, "is that Ms. Pewney defuse the device."

"Ms. Pewney?" I screeched. "With all due respect, Ms. Pewney, you're a great teacher, but … a bomb?"

"I wasn't always an English teacher, Timothy," said the woman lying at my feet. "Back in the day I was the best bomb disposal man the US Army had in Baghdad."

"So you've done this before?"

"Many times," she said. "It's been a few years, but disarming an IED is like riding a bicycle: you don't forget how to do it."

"If there's anything you need, …" Mr. Powers called.

"As a matter of fact, there is," the former best bomb disposal *man* in Baghdad answered. "Can you get me the flashlight from backstage? I'd ask Timothy, but ..." She finished her sentence with a chuckle.

Mr. Powers brought the flashlight and was promptly sent on his way. Although he protested, I thought I detected relief in his facial expression as he departed.

Ms. Pewney set to work immediately. So here I am, standing on the brightly lit stage of a darkened and empty auditorium, about to die. My only hope for survival is lying on her belly at my feet. And although it's not my entire life that's flashing in front of my eyes, the events that got me here are doing just that.

I tried to shake the images as best I could.

"Ms. Pewney?" I said. "Can I ask you something?" When she did not object, I continued, "When you said before that you were the best bomb disposal *man* in Baghdad, ..." I thought it impertinent to continue, and I certainly didn't wish to antagonize the person who was working to save my life, so I dropped my line of questioning and said, "Never mind. I'm sorry."

"No need to apologize, Timothy. As I said before, we all have a past." She looked up at me and smiled coyly.

"Does Mr. Powers know? I mean, about your being ... I mean, about your past?"

Removing the side panel of the stoop required concentration, so she didn't answer immediately. "Yes, Mr. Powers knows. Other than you, he's the only one."

"I'll make sure it stays that way," I said. The thought occurred to me that Ms. Pewney's secret might die with us.

My transgender English teacher was more concerned about the device she was attempting to disarm than about my preserving her secret, which was fine by me. After a moment of silence, she said, "You clever little devil."

"Erm, what did I do?"

Ms. Pewney erupted in a loud laugh. "Sorry, Timothy, I wasn't talking to you. I was talking to the bomb maker. The device you are standing on is fairly sophisticated."

"Is that supposed to make me feel better?" I asked. "Because it isn't working."

"Not to worry. I have everything under control. But I do need you to do something. Hand me that stack of index cards from the podium, would you? And try not to shift your weight when you pass them down."

I did as I was instructed, and Ms. Pewney jammed the index cards one at a time into something inside the wooden box underneath my feet. Then she said, "Now, Timothy, I need you to shift your weight very slowly onto your left foot. … That's good. … Easy. … Steady. … Now, when I count to three, I want you to lift your right leg completely off the platform, balance on your left leg until I say 'Jump,' at which point you jump off the stoop and hit the dirt—just in case. Have you got that?"

"Yes, ma'am!"

"One … two … three … and JUMP!"

I leapt to the floor and rolled away, fully expecting at the very least to lose a limb or two. Instead of the expected, deafening bang, all I heard was Ms. Pewney audibly exhaling. It was over.

The two of us picked ourselves up, dusted ourselves off, embraced for what seemed like several minutes, then began to laugh hysterically. When the police came, they saw a teenage boy and a middle-aged woman bouncing around the stage of an empty auditorium laughing like fools.

Epilogue

The Science Club's evolution lecture series got off to a late start—a day late, in fact. The police wouldn't let anyone enter the school building until they had conducted a thorough sweep in case there were more bombs. (There weren't.) After waiting for over two hours in the early-December cold without their jackets, neither students nor teachers were particularly interested in evolution—or learning of any kind—so Mr. Powers sent everyone home after lunch.

Fortunately, Cyrus Abrams had planned to spend the week with his daughter, so he was available to come and give his talk the next day. Interest in his talk was unprecedented, and it was broadcast on closed circuit TV throughout the school. Extracts, in fact, could be seen on national television that night and are still occasionally recycled when yet another discussion of the evolution "controversy" rears its ugly head somewhere.

I'm proud to say that my fellow Science Club members and I were nearly as brilliant as our guest speaker, even though we had to abbreviate our talks to make up for the fact that we only had three sessions rather than the originally planned four. (The Friday pep rally was, of course, sacrosanct.) Megan, in particular, excelled.

I am aware that everything I write from this point is anti-climactic, so I will be brief in finishing my tale. I have relegated a short (I promise!) summary of the science of evolution to an addendum.

The portrait of Batshit as given in national broadcasts and glossy magazine articles was less than favorable, which, I suppose, is only to be expected after an attempted assassination and a failed bombing. As a consequence of our town's besmirched image, my standing in the community is dubious, and visitors would be well advised to deny knowing me or even of me.

With the exception of the 'F' network and a few conservative print publications, the press portrayed the attempt by the Science Club to bring light into the darkness that is Batshit sympathetically. A well-known polling organization once again established that about four in ten adult Americans believe in creation as opposed to the scientifically accepted theory of evolution. (To my knowledge, there has never been a poll of Americans' acceptance of the theory of gravity.) That same organization also did some interesting polling at our school.

Before our lecture series began, exactly 30% of students at Omar L. Batshit High School believed the biblical version of creation to be "true" or "mostly true," while 54% believed in evolution by natural selection. The remaining 16% professed no preference. Attendees at our lectures were polled again afterwards, with rather interesting results: The number expressing no preference went down from 16% to a mere 4%. The number who accept evolution increased from 54% to 66%. Those readers with a mathematical bent will already have calculated that the percentage of believers in creation remained unchanged: 30% proved impervious to scientific reasoning.

On a more personal level, as of late February, Megan and I are still "an item," as my grandmother likes to put it. Grandma moved into the rather nice apartment above our garage a few weeks ago and is adjusting very nicely. She's a little old-fashioned about some things, though;

for example, she doesn't like to see my dad cooking and has virtually banned him from the kitchen. He says he doesn't mind because it gives him more time for his day trading and for his volunteer work, but Mother and I miss his cooking. (Grandma isn't a bad cook by any means, but she is far less adventurous than her son.)

GG hasn't expressed an opinion on the cooking question, but she is speaking more of late. I'm not sure if that's due to Zac's influence—she and Zac are still "together"—or Grandma's. Mands still doesn't say much, but, as she puts it, she talks when she has something to say, which seems like a sensible approach and one that I would like to recommend to quite a few people.

Josh came back to school after the Christmas break. He's even quieter and more studious than before. It must be hard having a dad in jail. There hasn't been a trial yet, only a few hearings, and Mr. Curtin was denied bail at all of them. His lawyer, radical attorney Veronica Langley-Thompson, wants him to plead insanity, but so far he prefers to use the courts and the press as pulpits for his bizarre version of Christianity. The news outlets are more than happy to oblige, and they regularly report his ramblings. Although Mr. Curtin has confessed to the attempted bombing as well, he can't possibly have placed the IED in the auditorium. The police are still looking for the perpetrator. They are convinced, by the way, that I wasn't the intended target of the IED; that does not make me feel better.

Stuart has undergone a transformation worthy of a butterfly. Ms. Pewney's coaching before the lecture series helped him gain some control over his jaw, and he seldom leaves his mouth hanging open and hardly ever drools. His part of the lectures went down well, and he has considerably more self-confidence than before.

Mike managed a C in every one of his subjects at the end of the first semester. He is no longer in danger of being thrown off the football team, which is a good thing, as he was named season MVP. Batshit

High finished the season with a decent record of eight wins and five losses. Coach Braun is already talking about division championships next year.

Mike and I only meet for tutoring three times a week now. Truth be told, he probably doesn't even need that much, but we both enjoy our sessions so much that it would be a shame to cut back more. We've become close friends, one might even say best friends. (Sorry, Josh.)

Coach Braun has taken to ignoring me. He has said he's grateful for my tutoring Mike, but he cannot get over the fact that I am, to put it mildly, not a natural athlete. (I have, however, improved considerably under Mike's tutelage and can now say that I actually enjoy—to a point—sports.)

Mrs. Barker is no longer at Batshit High. Just before Christmas she asked me to stay one day after class. "I won't be here after the holidays," she told me. "My work here is done."

"What do you mean?" I asked. Her sudden parting seemed to confirm Cyrus Abrams' suspicion that Mrs. Barker was a plant, there only for the purpose of inciting a lawsuit, but I wanted to hear it from her. Of course she was too clever to confirm that and too proud to deny it.

"You're smart. Figure it out," was her only answer. "But just so you know: I have a lot of respect for you. You're a lot like me."

"How so?"

"You stand up for what you believe in. You'll go far some day, Timothy."

ADDENDA

ADDENDUM 1: MOUSSE AU CHOCOLAT À LA DAD

It sounds a bit pretentious, I know, but "mousse au chocolat" (Say it: moose oh shaw-koh-LAH) is just another way of saying chocolate pudding. The only difference is that it's French and really, really good. This is how Dad makes it; he says it's based on a recipe by Martha Stewart, whoever that is.

> 6 oz. semi-sweet chocolate, broken into chunks
> 6 oz. butter (unsalted), cut into chunks
> ¼ cup strong coffee
> 4 eggs, separated (the bigger the better)
> ⅔ cup sugar plus 1 tbsp sugar
> 1 tbsp water
> pinch of salt
> ½ tsp vanilla extract
> large bowl of ice water

Melt the butter and chocolate together with the coffee in a double boiler. Dad says you can also use a bowl on top of a pot of boiling water, but then you have to be careful that none of the steam touches the chocolate because it "goes funny." I'm not the cook in our family, so I'll simply take his word for it.

Whisk the egg yolks with the ⅔ cup of sugar and the tablespoon of water in a bowl over the simmering bottom of your double boiler until it forms a thick mixture, about 3 minutes. (Dad says he adds "a swig" of rum or cognac at this point if no minors are among the guests.)

Place the bowl with the egg mixture into the ice water and continue beating until cool and thick. Fold in the chocolate mixture.

In another bowl—no wonder our dishwasher always seems to be running—beat the egg whites with the salt until they are "good and frothy" and start to hold their shape. Whip in the tablespoon of sugar, then the vanilla extract.

Fold the egg white mixture gently into the chocolate mixture, "but don't overdo it."

Fill into a serving dish or individual bowls and refrigerate for 4 or more hours.

Dad usually serves the mousse with a little whipped cream on the side. *Bon appétit!*

ADDENDUM 2: DAD'S POTATOES DAUPHINOISE

Another French recipe—I guess they're good cooks, the French. Dad says he got this from "one of the guys at the homeless shelter." (It doesn't taste like something a homeless person would eat, much less make.) The name is pronounced doe-feen-WAHZ, by the way.

- 4 **medium potatoes**
- 1 **tbsp butter**
- 3 **cloves of garlic, finely chopped**
  salt and pepper
  nutmeg
- 1 **cup cream**
- 1 **cup milk**
- 1 **cup grated cheese ("whatever I have around, usually cheddar or gruyere")**

Grease an ovenproof dish. Spread the chopped garlic around the bottom and sides of the dish.

Peel and thinly slice the potatoes.

Put a layer of potato slices along the bottom of the dish, overlapping them slightly.

Season the layer with salt, pepper and nutmeg.

Repeat the layering and seasoning until you've used all your potatoes.

Combine the cream and the milk, then pour over the potatoes. Dad says you might have to wedge up the potatoes a little to allow the liquid to get in between.

Bake at 350°F (175°C) for about an hour, then sprinkle the grated cheese over the top and bake for 20 to 30 minutes more, until the top is "nice and brown."

Looks best if served in neat wedges, "but that doesn't always work out." Enjoy!

ADDENDUM 3: EVOLUTION IN A NUTSHELL

Believe me, trying to debate a creationist is an exercise in futility. I've tried. These people have made up their minds, and they're not interested in logical discussion. You will not convince them, but others listening to you will probably recognize that you have the facts on your side. So here are the facts; there's no room to present the proof here, but at the end I'll recommend some books that will help if you ever find yourself in need of assistance convincing a skeptic of one of the most widely accepted theories in all of science.

The earth is, as my math teacher surreptitiously wrote on the board, about 4.54 billion years old. That time scale is consistent with the ages of meteorites and lunar samples, all as determined by radiometric age dating.

Life started to form on earth about 3.7 billion years ago. The exact mechanisms that led to the first one-celled life forms aren't entirely clear, but some combination of chemical reactions and possibly lightning strikes caused the first life cell to form in what is known as the "primordial soup," the gases and liquids that were present on the surface of the early earth.

The primitive, one-celled life forms that grew in the primordial soup were the ancestors of every living thing—plant or animal—on earth today. Scientists talk of "common ancestry." That's why a fairly high percentage of the DNA in all life forms is identical.

It's possible to trace back the development of lots of species by looking at what geologists call the "fossil record." The earth's crust shows layers, the deepest ones being the oldest. Looking back at fossils found in the different layers, paleontologists (geologists who study fossils) can see how species changed over time.

Charles Darwin was the first one to publish a comprehensive theory about the processes that cause species to change: they adapt to their environments over time. This is known as evolution.

Evolution is a random process: an animal is born with a mutation, and the environment determines whether the mutation is a good thing or not. For example, when Darwin sailed around the Galapagos Islands off South America on board the *Beagle*, he observed that certain birds, a kind of finch we now know as the Darwin finch, looked very different on different islands. On one island they had hefty beaks that helped them crack seeds; on another island they had long beaks that allowed them to reach between the spikes of a cactus and pick out insects that were hiding there. It all depended on what kind of food was available on the island.

Darwin figured out that there was a process going on that is known as "natural selection." If a bird was born with a longer, thinner beak, that bird did well on an island with cacti, but died on an island that had only hard seeds that needed to be cracked. The birds that did well had offspring, and their offspring looked like them; the dead birds obviously had no offspring, so eventually each island had only one kind of bird. Darwin spoke of "survival of the fittest": those that were most fit—i.e. best adapted—for life in a particular environment were the ones that survived.

These processes can be observed happening all the time. In some species evolution happens very fast because the species reproduce very quickly. Flu viruses, for example, evolve from one flu season to the next. In other species, evolution is very slow: humans don't reproduce so quickly, so we cannot see how our species is evolving. That doesn't mean it isn't happening.

Selected Bibliography

If you ever want to get beyond the basics I presented in the last addendum, you might want to have a look at some of these books. And if your school librarian is even half as helpful as Miss Abrams, he or she might be able to recommend newer and/or better sources.

Daniel Loxton: *Evolution. How We and All Living Things Came to Be.* Kids Can Press, Toronto, 2010.

This is a great introduction for the budding scientist—I'd have probably read it in the 4th grade, but I suspect it's at the junior high level. It takes the reader very clearly and logically through the science, from how life first came about to critical questions about evolution (and how to answer them).

Jay Hosler: *Evolution: The Story of Life on Earth.* Hill and Wang, New York, 2011.

In the form of a graphic novel, aliens learn about life on earth. Not really my cup of tea, but I suspect it would be excellent reading for non-scientists who want to painlessly learn about the subject.

Neil Shubin: *Your Inner Fish: A Journey into the 3.5-Billion-Year History of the Human Body.* Pantheon, New York, 2008.

This one reads almost like a detective novel, but it gives great information on both evolution and how paleontologists work. A good read for interested students and adults alike.

Jerry A. Coyne: *Why Evolution Is True.* Penguin Books, New York, 2010.

This is probably the best case ever made to *prove* that evolution is a fact. It's fairly long and involved, so I wouldn't recommend it unless you're really serious about the subject.

Mark Isaac: *The Counter-Creationism Handbook.* University of California Press, Berkeley, 2007.

This one gives you an answer to just about any conceivable argument a creationist (or ID proponent) could possibly come up with, over 400 in all. Be warned: It's heavy on the science, and no coincidence that it was published by a university press. I understood it, of course, but I'd only recommend it for science teachers, school administrators, school board members and so on who have to deal with the crusaders of ignorance on a fairly regular basis.

Eugenie C. Scott: *Evolution vs. Creationism: An Introduction.* University of California Press, Berkeley, 2009.

Another university press publication, so again not for the faint of heart. This goes into the societal and legal aspects of the debate, including an interesting history of the subject. If I hadn't read this, I'd never have been prepared for some of the weirder arguments against evolution: who'd have known you could bring Hitler into the discussion, for example?

About the Author

Allen J. Woppert was born and raised in Milwaukee, Wisconsin, and earned a BA from the University of Wisconsin's Madison campus.

Allen spent his junior year of college abroad, studying in Bonn, Germany. After graduating college, he spent a year teaching in the U.S. before returning to Germany to teach English. He carried his know-how as an English teacher into his writing career to author or co-author dozens of textbooks and short works of fiction intended to help people learn English.

Allen has now turned to writing short stories and young adult novels, including some set in schools and other educational settings. He calls upon his firsthand understanding of classroom dynamics to create rich, believable scenarios in his fiction.

When not writing, Allen likes to travel. He has seen much of Europe as well as North and South America (and small parts of Asia and Africa). His favorite places include Peru, where he lived and traveled for several months, and the Galapagos Islands, which he visited on the trail of Darwin.

Connect with the author online
www.allenwoppert.com

Learn more about the Town of Batshit
www.batshit.com

Made in the USA
Charleston, SC
07 November 2013